THE WITCH HUNTERS

You are so there.

T•WITCHES

T•WITCHES

H.B. GILMOUR
& RANDI REISFELD

SCHOLASTIC INC.

NEW YORK   TORONTO   LONDON   AUCKLAND   SYDNEY
MEXICO CITY   NEW DELHI   HONG KONG   BUENOS AIRES

ISBN 0-439-49227-0

12 11 10 9 8 7 6 5 4 3   3 4 5 6 7 8/0

PRINTED IN THE U.S.A.   40
FIRST PRINTING, JUNE 2003

DEDICATION

For John and Jessi, with love
— H.B.G.

THE WITCH HUNTERS

CHAPTER ONE
BASH OF THE CENTURY

One minute Camryn Barnes was chilling in a white stretch limousine, listening to the excited babbling of her best buds as they cruised toward the gala opening of a star-studded movie in Boston.

The next, she was chilled to the bone, spinning out of control, watching helplessly as a dark car sped wildly toward the limo, set to demolish it and all its giddy passengers.

"Stop!" Cam screamed, bolting upright.

Her friends turned to stare at her openmouthed.

The limo's black-capped chauffeur, separated from his passengers by a sliding soundproof window, hadn't heard her. Without so much as tapping the brakes, he continued straight for the deadly intersection.

To ordinary eyes, the road ahead looked safe.

Cam alone had seen what was coming.

Her heart lurched, her head throbbed, even as she realized that the car she had pictured was nowhere in sight.

It would be. Any minute. Cam struggled frantically to open her seat belt. Finally, leaping forward, she elbowed aside her sister and her friends Amanda and Sukari, who sat facing her on the jump seats. "You have to stop! Right now!" she ordered the chauffeur, as she pounded on the thick plastic barrier.

She was alone no longer. One other person now knew, believed, got it.

Alexandra Fielding, Cam's identical but temperamentally opposite twin, grasped her sister's elbow. *Easy, girl, you're having a premonition, a vision. What do you see?* At hyper-speed, Alex sent rather than spoke the question in the crowded limo.

There's a car heading right for us! Cam's desperate mind answered.

Who, where, what? Alex demanded, as talented at "hearing" thoughts as Cam was at "seeing" what loomed ahead.

I can't make it out that clearly, Cam wailed telepathically, beginning to shake now. *A dark car at a four-way intersection. It's going to barrel through the stop sign and totally take us out!*

At that moment, Alex heard it.

The roaring engine.

The squeal of tires taking a corner at hazardous speed.

The crash-car driver's voice — no, his thoughts, furious, ferocious — *Brice Stanley, the end is near! Warlock, your time has come!*

Her sharply honed senses caught a scent of something nauseating. . . . Eau de toxic dump site mixed with . . . rotten eggs. The car's reckless driver reeked of the stuff.

It's happening! Cam screamed telepathically. She was sitting now, her hands trembling as she snapped shut her seat belt. *We're gonna get rammed!*

Would it be faster to *will* the thick barrier between the chauffeur and them to shatter, to telekinetically break through the soundproof divider? Alex squeezed her eyes shut and focused all her energy on the partition. She imagined it exploding. And, as it did, she screamed to the startled driver, "Now! Hit the brakes! This minute!!"

Shaken, the chauffeur responded mechanically, his hands jerking the steering wheel, his foot heavy on the brake. The limo went into a tailspin and Cam's friends Brianna, Kristen, Beth, and Cam herself jolted forward on their white leather seat, saved from flying forward only by their seat belts. The others, Alex, Amanda, and Sukari, who sat facing them, bounced hard, too. The car behind them screeched to a stop, inches from the rear bumper of the limo, setting off a chain of blaring horns and shouting drivers.

And the dark car Cam had seen shot through the intersection — the intersection they would have been smack in the middle of if the chauffeur hadn't automatically obeyed Alex's desperate command.

As the dark car swept past in a blur, Alex smelled it again, stronger this time — the rancid cheese and acid stench of a lab experiment gone wrong.

The stretch limo's passengers had been screaming from the moment the chauffeur jammed on the brakes. As the long white car came out of its final spin, their panicked screams of "Oh, my god!" "What's going on?" and "Help, help!" slowly faded to hyperventilating gasps of "Are you all right?" "What just happened?" and "That was close."

Sukari, her normally confident voice reduced to a whisper, turned to Cam. "How did you know?"

"The question is . . ." Brianna began. Brianna Waxman, whose father had sent his limo for them, pretended that she'd fully recovered and fell into default bossy mode.

Flicking back her expensively highlighted blond hair, she demanded, "How do you *always* know?"

Beth Fish sighed. Of all Cam's friends, Beth had been her tightest bud since kindergarten. The girl with the dark curls and knee-jerk loyalty tried to lighten the intense moment. "Cam's mojo strikes again."

"Mojo" her crew called it.

Not magick.

Cam tried to hang on to her shaky smile, tried to hide her distress from her buds. No matter how many times she'd "guessed right" about things, they'd never believe that she could actually picture events before they happened, that she was often overwhelmed by weird, mind-blowing, migraine-bestowing hunches, signs, and premonitions.

They wouldn't have believed it even if she told them. She was a witch. And so was Alex.

Apple-cheeked Amanda never questioned Cam's "amazing intuition," or how often her hunches turned out to be on the money. "Of course she knew," the candle-lighting, incense-burning redhead explained, as if it were completely obvious. "It's her karma. In a past life, Cam was probably saved from some major disaster and now it's her karma to protect others."

Alex interjected wryly, "Everyone who thinks, 'Who

cares how Cam knew, let's just be glad we're not road-kill,' please raise her hand."

"This is all sooo beside the point!" Bummed about being out of the spotlight for a moment, Bree rolled her emerald eyes. "We're on our way to preview a movie that is totally slated for megahit status. Not only did my daddy produce *The Witching Hour*, but — hello! — it stars Brice Stanley, the buff, blue-eyed, two-time Academy Award–nominated Hollywood hottie! So anyone who's thinking, 'Mojo-shmojo, let's just go,' please wave those digits."

Everyone's hands flew up, except for Kristen Hsu's. Bree glared at her best bud. Kristen's olive skin was drained of color, and her hands were clapped over her mouth. "I think I'm gonna hurl right now," she finally blurted.

"Not in my daddy's car!" Bree warned.

Everything was moving fast. Way too fast, Cam thought, as the limo continued its journey.

Just two weeks ago, she and Alex had been racing through the haunted forests of Coventry Island. Tiny, re-mote, hidden from the Wisconsin mainland by fog and distance, Coventry — or Witch Island, as the locals called it — was where Cam and Alex had been born.

Though they had literally never set foot on the is-land until then.

Taken from Coventry when they were infants, too young to walk or even crawl, the twins were reared by different families.

Neither had known of the other's existence for fourteen years.

Then, two weeks ago, they had returned to their mysterious birthplace — Alex practically dancing with excitement; Cam's heels weighted with dread — for the funeral of the beloved warlock who had protected and guided them all their lives.

Lord Karsh Antayus.

Karsh had reluctantly helped separate them as infants, then mischievously maneuvered to bring them together again as teens.

Now here they were in Massachusetts, nearly a thousand miles from Wisconsin and a world away from Coventry, in a white stretch limo on their way to see a hot new movie starring Brice Stanley — who only *they* knew was a warlock.

Only they, and the maniac driving the car that had nearly killed them.

CHAPTER TWO
THE WITCHING HOUR

Bright lights crisscrossed the sky. Traffic slowed. The shrieks and screams of the frantic crowd grew deafening.

The near-miss accident had delayed the girls' arrival, and Bree, for one, intended to make up for lost time. Clambering over Kristen's poufy taffeta skirt, the beaming blond was first out of the limo. She could barely wait for her friends before making a mad dash toward the scene. Her stiletto heels didn't slow her down a bit. Nor did the thousands of fans already stationed on either side of a roped-off red carpet.

The Six Pack quickly caught up with her. "How are we even gonna get close now?" Kristen whined.

Undaunted, Bree announced, "Follow the leader. I've got it all under control." Approaching a security guard on crowd-control duty, she whipped out the invitation that had been sent to the lucky VIPs. "Excuse me, sir," she confidently chirped, "I'm Eric Waxman's daughter —"

The rent-a-cop shrugged, seriously unimpressed.

"The executive producer of the movie? Hello?" Bree pointed to the words on the invite and read, "Eric Waxman invites you —" The man was staring at the card but Bree rushed on, "See, my friends and I are supposed to be right up front. My daddy will be so upset if he doesn't see me there, so can you just escort us?"

Cam didn't know if it was Bree's smile, her *chutzpah,* or the cop's easy dupe-ability, but he guided the girls through the throng and, displacing fans who'd claimed that spot, cleared a space in the front.

Just then, someone shouted, "He's here! He's here —"

He was, too. As if by magic, the brightest spotlight fell on Brice Stanley, illuminating his megawatt smile and sparkling blue eyes. Dressed in a pricey designer suit but oozing down-home charm, the charismatic star waved, turning to include everyone. "Hello, Boston!" he shouted enthusiastically. "Thank you from the bottom of my heart for coming out to support *The Witching Hour.* You guys are the best!"

The fandemonium ramped up, and Brice started up the red carpet toward the theater. As expected of the rakishly handsome star, he stopped often to autograph pictures thrust at him, shake outstretched hands, wink at swooning admirers, accept bouquets of flowers.

While Alex silently gave Brice props for his preshow performance, it was the woman at his side who caught her attention. She whispered, "Cam, check out Brice's date. Is she someone I should know?"

Alex was celebrity-impaired, but even Cam did not recognize the tall, serious-looking brunette at Brice's side. Her arm was around his waist, but her keen, intelligent eyes kept scanning the crowd, as if she was looking for someone.

"Something's off —" Cam started to say.

"What, you really expected him to bring Ileana?" Alex finished the sentence Cam hadn't even realized she'd been thinking.

One of Coventry Island's most brilliant and beautiful witches, Ileana was their cousin — and their moody, demanding guardian — and not so incidentally, Brice Stanley's girlfriend.

"There's my father!" Brianna shrieked, jumping up and down and waving madly. "Daddy, Daddy!" Her shrill screams caused Six Pack heads to turn as one. Even Cam and Alex looked over.

And there, in the roped-off VIP area, was Mr. Waxman, preening in the limelight his daughter craved. Two celebrities flanked the short, trim, tuxedoed producer — a curvy, silver-gowned brunette, who played a brilliant lawyer on one of TV's top shows, and a stout, smiling U.S. senator, easily three times Bree's dad's size.

The starlet and the senator waved back at the girls; Eric Waxman nodded curtly, looking annoyed at the interruption.

Disappointed and deflated, Bree scrambled for a way to take charge again. Only this time, her moment was ruined by something far more disturbing than a diss by Daddy Dearest.

Alex heard it a microsecond before everyone else. She wheeled around to see someone swathed in black, forcing his way through the tightly packed fans.

"Ouch! Hey . . . what are you . . . what th —" Ripples of startled annoyance came from the outer edge of the crowd, getting closer, louder, and angrier as . . . a tall figure, his face hidden by the hood of a long, dark cape, crashed through the mob, oblivious of who he jostled, elbowed, and trampled in his path.

The hooded man was determined to barrel his way to the front, heading, in fact, toward the exact spot where Cam, Alex, and their friends were waiting to greet Brice.

Cam might have reacted sooner, had she not been hit with the sudden sweating, chills, fever, dizziness, and blurry vision that signaled something major was about to happen. Something bad.

By the time she and Alex did react, the weirdo was almost on them. He was carrying a strange, curved blade on a long handle. The crowd parted before him, people ducking instinctively, shielding their heads with their arms. But the fans who had turned out for Brice's premiere were not his target.

Brice was.

"Warlock, your time has come!" the madman bellowed.

Waving the weapon, he rushed toward Brice — pausing for a moment at the gold rope holding the crowd back from the red carpet. "Brice Stanley is a witch!" he hollered to the assembled fans. "Brice Stanley, role model to millions, is a fraud. He lives a lie. He is a warlock and you, all of you" — the head inside the hood rotated to take in the stunned horde — "are fools, dupes, and worse, to worship this twisted man, this evil warlock."

Maybe it was his out-of-nowhere appearance or his over-the-top ranting, but Bree suddenly began to giggle, loudly and nervously. Pointing at the man making his way toward the red carpet, she announced, "Leave it to my daddy to plant someone as a publicity ploy."

Kristen, Beth, and Amanda turned their terrified eyes to her, wondering for a second whether she could be right.

"If that's what's up," Kristen ventured, "the caped creep is a really good actor!"

"You think?" Beth was dubious but decided to go down that road. It was easier and better than other possibilities. "He's wearing a hooded black robe and carrying a scary . . . a scythe, I think it's called, or a sickle —"

"He looks just like one of my tarot cards," Amanda broke in, unsteadily and unconvinced.

"Well, Honor Roll, what's he supposed to be?" Bree turned to Cam for an answer. Before she could speak, Sukari nailed it.

"Death," she said.

The hooded figure carrying the scythe made his way toward the barricade holding back the fans.

Stop him, Cam thought she heard a voice command.

She turned to Alex. But her sister was intensely focused on the cloaked stranger.

"Did you say something?" Cam whispered.

The man whirled, his cape flaring, his weapon whistling through the air.

Alex! Cam silently implored. *This is no stunt — it's*

*the guy who almost smashed into us! He must have
been rushing to get here.*

Her sister was already on the case.

And so was Brice's gal-pal, who spun suddenly, a
gun in her hand.

What's she doing with a gun? Cam telegraphed.
There's a crowd here. She can't shoot.

You take the gun, I'm on the scythe, Alex responded.

Cam reached for the necklace she always wore.
Clutching her sun charm, she turned her gray-eyed gaze
on the handgun in the grasp of the strange woman. As she
stared at the cold steel, warmth rose in her gut, her neck
grew hot, her extraordinary eyes began to sting and
tear . . . and then the barrel of the pistol started to bubble
and hiss. Under Cam's spell, the weapon had begun to melt.

Alex was having a harder time honing in on the
scythe. The moment she closed her eyes, a putrid, sulfur-
tinged stench assaulted her.

"Hold it right there!" Brice's date was hollering at
the hooded man. The tip of her gun glowed red, the steel
still crackling under Cam's glare. "Security! Stop where
you are!" she called.

The weird, costumed stranger paid no attention to
the undercover security woman's orders. Instead, he

brought the scythe down on the security rope, slashing it in half.

Stalking steadily toward Brice, he chanted, "Confess, warlock, cohort of witches! The Witch Hunter has come. Brice Stanley, your secret is safe no more!"

With her furious will, Alex ignored her nausea and concentrated on picturing the man's hands . . . as they unwillingly loosened their grip on the scythe's handle. She imagined that handle lifting off like the tail of a rocket . . . saw it sailing far above the hysterical crowd. It vaulted into the flawless blue sky, curving like the McDonald's arches until it disappeared with a loud clatter into the alley behind the theater.

The stunned stalker whirled toward Cam and Alex. Behind them, Beth, Kristen, Bree, and Sukari held on to each other, completely weirded out.

Mouths and eyes wide open, all the fans had followed the scythe's flight. "I knew it," people began to say, laughing, some rising from crouched positions. "*The Witching Hour,* get it? It was a gag, a publicity stunt!"

And in that moment, though she could still see him, Alex knew he was history. The robed-and-hooded freak barreled through the crowd, sending a silent threat in Cam and Alex's direction. *Witches, you are next. All three of you!*

Woozy from their efforts, Cam and Alex turned to each other. "I heard him, Alex. He was talking to us," Cam whispered.

"Yeah, and I . . . It's so weird, Cami . . . I *saw* him without, like, actually *seeing* him," Alex said. "He's in his car right now, the one that nearly creamed us. He's gone."

The security woman dropped her now-useless gun, which Cam suddenly realized was not filled with metal-jacketed bullets but with tranquilizer cartridges. It had grown too hot to hold, too twisted to fire. She had no idea what had gone wrong with her weapon.

Three uniformed guards now flanked Brice Stanley. Just before they rushed him into the theater, the star shot a grateful smile at Cam and Alex.

"You so owe me," Bree announced to the Six Pack, confident her guess was right. "I mean, you did see that, didn't you? Thanks to my daddy, Brice Stanley just grinned directly at us!"

CHAPTER THREE
A SPELLBINDING CELEBRITY

"He's doing it again," Amanda whispered, pressing Sukari's hand so hard her friend yipped.

"He is, he is," Kristen told Bree. "He's looking at us again."

The movie was over and most of the invited guests had left the theater. A dozen or so people still sat, some standing now, stretching, in the section that had been reserved for VIPs. Brice Stanley was among them. The star was shaking hands, receiving hugs, and, yes, Amanda was right. Brice Stanley kept glancing over at the girls and grinning.

Cam, who could read her sister's mind but no one

else's, thought she heard his voice. "Als, is he saying something?" she whispered to her twin. "I mean, did he just send a message?"

Alex confirmed it. "He said we should stay for a minute, wait until the others are outside. He wants to talk with us."

"Alex, I heard him!" Cam confided. But when her sister looked at her doubtfully, she added, "Just softly, just the sound of his voice, not the actual words —"

"Daddy, Daddy!" Bree was standing on her seat, balancing herself with a hand on Kristen's shoulder. Mr. Waxman rushed to where the girls were waiting.

"Down, down," he hissed. "Don't embarrass me —"

"*Down?*" Beth whispered angrily to Cam. "He sounds like he's talking to a dog."

Bree reddened and scrambled miserably from her perch. Alex wished she hadn't been able to read the crushed girl's mind; she felt like a mental gate-crasher as Bree's desperate thoughts reached her. *Oh, no. Why can't I ever do anything right around him? Now he'll never invite me to anything again.*

It didn't take a witch to know how bad Bree was feeling. Sukari, who was nearly a head taller than Mr. Waxman, stepped between Bree and her dad, hiding her crestfallen friend, giving Bree a chance to repair her ego privately.

"Mr. W. Nice movie," the plump, cocoa-skinned girl told their host, studying him the way she would a lab rat. "I bet it'll be a blockbuster when it comes out on DVD. Oh, and thanks for the limo you sent for us. It was so . . . white —"

"What do you mean, when it comes out on DVD?" Eric Waxman anxiously demanded. "What about theaters? It's slated for national release next Friday —"

"Hi! Which one of you is Bree?" Brice Stanley's mischievous grin moved across the Six Pack like a dazzling klieg light.

"Me!" Kristen shouted, losing her mind and raising her hand.

Sukari stepped out of Bree's way.

"I mean, she is!" Kristen quickly regrouped, pushing her best friend forward.

At a very non-Bree loss for words, the petite girl held out her hand.

Brice took it, covered it with his other hand, and held on. "So you're Brianna?" he said. "Your father can't stop bragging about you."

"He brags about me?" Bree breathed.

"Says you're his finest production," Brice assured her. "Right, Eric?"

"Whatever you say, Brice." Bree's dad reached up to slap the movie star's broad shoulder. "DVD?" He shook his head at Sukari. "You wouldn't pay box office bucks, but you'd rent it? DVDs!"

But Suke was ignoring him now. Like all the girls, she couldn't help being enthralled by Brice's spellbinding smile.

An assistant came up, holding a pile of promotional videos about *The Witching Hour*, and began handing them out to the girls.

"What are you doing?" Waxman whirled on him.

"You said DVDs, but I figured you meant these videos. I heard you," the young man answered.

"They're for VIPs," Eric Waxman scolded. "I mean —" He quickly changed his tone in front of Brice. "For journalists. Anyway, they already saw the movie, right? And this one" — he jerked his head in Sukari's direction — "would rather spend her allowance at Blockbuster, anyway."

Brice took a few videos and a felt-tipped marker from Waxman's assistant. He began autographing the tapes and handing them out to the Six Pack.

"What happened before the movie?" It was Beth. "Who was the creep in the costume?"

"And the girl with the gun?" Kristen added.

"A joke, a shtick. Just something to keep the crowd amused. It was a publicity stunt," Eric Waxman hurriedly answered.

"A publicity stunt?" Show-me girl Sukari was skeptical. "With a gun?"

"Uh, it was a fake — plastic."

"Yeah, but the guy with the scythe" — Amanda piped up — "if it was a publicity stunt, I don't get it. I mean, aside from the title, the movie had nothing to do with witches or warlocks or tarot cards —"

"A stunt, that's all. Some idiot publicity guy's idea of a joke," Eric Waxman insisted. "Come on, let's get back to the limo. Brice has had a long day."

Only two of the girls hadn't received copies of the movie — Cam and Alex. "They'll be right with you, as soon as I autograph their videos," Brice promised, as Mr. Waxman hustled the others toward the exit.

"Ileana's description was perfect." He looked from one twin to the other. "I'm so glad to finally meet you —"

"Oh, me, too," Cam said unexpectedly and, Alex thought, a bit awestuck.

"It wasn't a publicity stunt." Alex cut to the chase, though, truth be told, her own heart was doing the butterfly flutter. Brice was not just movie-star hot — there was an aura of strength mixed with good-guy sweetness about him that could melt the chocolate off a DoveBar.

"That's your professional opinion?" he asked now, as if he were talking to an equal.

"It was no stunt," Cam said without hesitation.

"The caped crusader was for real," Alex confirmed.

"He was. And is. He's been sending me threats for years. Me, and others like me — like us," Brice generously corrected himself. "Mostly, those among us who are in the public eye —"

"You mean witches and warlocks." Cam wanted to get it straight.

Brice nodded. "He calls himself 'the Witch Hunter.' And he practically announced that he'd show up tonight. I think he misunderstood the film's title, assumed it was some epic in praise of witches. *The Witching Hour* just means the time when something important will change. Of course, I told Eric . . . your friend Brianna's father . . . that I'd been getting these weird letters. He didn't want the police involved, so he arranged for private security —"

"Posing as your date?" Alex asked sheepishly.

"Yes. That was my bright idea." He shook his head and bestowed one of his killer grins on them. "If I'd known how talented, how adept you two are, I wouldn't have needed security, would I?"

Cam blushed, then asked, "How dangerous is he, Brice, uh, Mr. Stanley?"

"Brice," Brice said.

"He was carrying that . . . scythe —" Cam added. "He was dressed as Death."

"Death? I thought it was Father Time — all that ranting about 'Your time has come!' To answer your question honestly — before tonight, I hadn't given him that much credibility. But you guys really feel he's dangerous?" Brice was taking them seriously.

"Totally," Alex jumped in. "Right before he disappeared, he cursed us. Threatened us. He said, 'You're next. All three of you.'"

"*And* he tried to run us down. On our way to the premiere, he nearly rammed our limo," Cam confided with a shudder.

Brice watched them for a moment — long enough for Alex to hear his thoughts and puff up with pride. *They're good,* she heard him thinking. *Ileana was right. Their instincts are terrifically sharp.*

"So far, he's seemed more rash, more reckless and unpredictable, than dangerous," he finally said. "But he may be more trouble than I thought." Then he told them what he knew of the Witch Hunter.

The man was a fanatic. Someone who feared and hated witches. Probably, Brice thought, because of something personal, something that had happened to him that had scared him.

He had been sending menacing notes to many in the entertainment community, calling them witches, threatening to "out" them, to reveal their secret to the world. There were plenty of maniacs who did that, Brice told them. The problem was, this one had the shrewdness or sensitivity to recognize true witches, to actually know the ones in his midst. Which meant that the Witch Hunter had some advanced skill; if he was not a witch himself, then the man had a degree of sensitivity beyond that of an everyday person. A sixth sense, a superior level of ESP . . .

Like Dave, Cam immediately thought. Her adoptive father was a "Sensitive," a person with highly developed intuition and abilities. That's why he had been chosen to be her Protector.

"Do you have any idea who he meant when he said 'All three of you'?" Brice asked, startling her.

"You, of course," Alex answered. But then she thought for a second. "No, wait, the dude said that to *us*. You were over on the red carpet."

As Brice nodded, Cam remembered something else. Just before the Witch Hunter broke through the security barricade, she'd heard someone urge, *Stop him!* Now she realized it hadn't been Alex. It had come from someone else in the crowd, someone standing very near them.

CHAPTER FOUR
A MATTER OF TRUST

"How dare he!" Ileana's fury at Brice Stanley was out of control. The magnificent, miffed witch was all about destruction now. Metallic-gray eyes flashing, she zeroed in on a cherished photo of her boyfriend, the movie star. Once, all she'd had to do was glare at it — and the autographed eight-by-ten glossy would have gone up in flames. But she couldn't do that now.

Ileana had lost her witchy powers.

But not her witchy temper.

Jaws clenched, she jerked the smiling picture out of its frame. "How could he do this" — she hissed, tearing the photo in half — "to *me*?!"

As she spun around, another image of Brice taunted her — the picture on the cover of the *Coventry Island Tattler.* There he was, beaming in the spotlight at the premiere of *The Witching Hour.* At his side, her arm snaked around his waist, stood . . . another woman.

Ileana could not deal with the accompanying article. She didn't want to know the name of Brice's new gal-pal or any details of what should have been her night.

Brice Stanley had asked *her* to the premiere, then, at the very last minute, canceled their date.

Flabbergasted as Ileana had been, she'd managed to pathetically screech, "Why?"

To which he'd replied, just before hanging up, "Trust me."

Like the talon-sharp claws of a bird of prey, Ileana's fingers swooped down on the newspaper image of her erstwhile squeeze. She balled it up in her fist and hurled it across the room.

Enough. There was something she needed to take care of — something far more important than her twisted, two-timing, "trust me" ex!

There was an urgent matter. Of immense importance.

Just thinking of it, Ileana's heart, which had been racing with rage, was now seized with dread.

Someone had stolen the journal her wise and loving

guardian had entrusted to her. It was as irreplaceable as the good warlock who'd written it. Karsh. In his shaky scrawl, he had recorded the secrets of generations. And with his dying breath, he had beseeched Ileana to read what he'd set down.

Of course she had.

And left the journal in a safe place, too. Inside the hollowed-out book where Karsh had hidden it. In her own home. Beside her bed. On the nightstand.

The nightstand that now held another treasured gift. The crystal perfume bottle Brice Stanley had given to her. It had belonged to his mother and, before that, his grandmother.

But the book had disappeared.

With fresh frustration, the thwarted witch glared at the priceless flask. She wanted it out — out of her sight, out of her life.

Under her angry gaze, the heirloom flask shattered, raining crystal across the floor.

Ileana jumped back, gasping in horror. She hadn't really meant to destroy it. More to the point, with her powers gone to seed, she hadn't really known she could.

A feathery voice wafted into her room. "Silly girl. He was trying to protect you."

Ileana spun toward the bedroom door. How long had Miranda been there, watching her? Miranda DuBaer, the twins' mother, was still regal in her bearing, despite the painful exile she'd suffered.

"Protect me? From his cheating. I was supposed to be there!" the blond beauty sputtered. "He broke our date. To be with that . . . that —"

"Security guard," Miranda broke in, matter-of-factly. "You never bothered to read the *Tattler* piece, did you? You saw the picture and freaked out." She picked up the newspaper Ileana had hurled into a corner and, smoothing its crumpled pages, began to read the article aloud.

"So she wasn't really his date. Fine." The flustered witch crossed her arms, still not satisfied. So Brice had known a maniac dedicated to exposing him might show up. Why hadn't he confided in her? Did he think she was untrustworthy? That she couldn't keep a secret?

"Secret?" Miranda echoed. "Speaking of — I found no journal at Crailmore."

Crailmore was the home of Ileana's despicable father. "You've searched Thantos's fortress?" the tempestuous witch asked.

"Neither he nor Karsh's book is there." Miranda settled into an overstuffed chair and watched her reckless niece pace the room. "Ileana, why do we need the journal? We know . . . you've told me . . . what the book contains. Why must we find it?"

"I didn't tell you everything," Ileana confessed,

flouncing into a chair across from the serene, auburn-haired witch.

She had explained the Antayus Curse to Miranda, an oath spat out in pain and hatred hundreds of years before that condemned to early death every male head of the DuBaer family. The curse, Karsh had written, had not skipped a generation since the Salem Witch Trials.

But she hadn't confided what Karsh Antayus and his dear friend Nathaniel DuBaer, father of the devious Thantos, had settled on to end the bloodletting.

That from their generation on, only women would rule the dynasty.

DuBaer women.

And that meant that Apolla and Artemis — Camryn and Alexandra — Miranda's daughters and Ileana's treasured charges, should rightfully head the clan.

Thantos knew and denied this. It was the secret that, once revealed, would wrench away his control over the limitless wealth and power of the DuBaers.

But only Karsh's account, set down in his own hand, could prove it.

No one in all of Coventry would believe the words of impetuous Ileana or the once-mad mother of the twins, Miranda.

"All right." Miranda easily read Ileana's mind and sighed resignedly. "In that case, we must . . . we will . . .

find the journal. But if Karsh knew of this curse, why didn't he proclaim it long ago and stop Thantos from taking what wasn't his?" she wondered aloud, just as a lightning bolt of truth hit her. At the time, there were no DuBaer women to stand in Thantos's way. Now there were two of them —

Ileana confirmed it. "Once Camryn and Alex are initiated, they must begin to fulfill their destiny. Thantos never feared either of them when they were alone and separated."

"But," Miranda interrupted, "he believed they had died."

That was the big lie, Ileana wanted to scream, he used to keep you docile, under his control. She didn't say it, though, knowing Miranda would never accept that truth — not until she could prove it.

Ileana continued, "Anyway, only together were they strong enough to outsmart him. And only after their initiation will they — together — be powerful enough to overthrow him. That's why he never wanted them brought together. And precisely why Karsh did."

Once, before the twins were born, Miranda had taken the motherless Ileana under her wing. That long-ago mother–daughter bond had recently re-formed into one of friendship. Now Miranda walked to where the young witch sat and perched on the arm of her chair.

"Thantos has a lot to lose if Karsh's journal proves him an imposter. He must have stolen the book."

"No way would His Lordship stoop to petty thievery," Ileana countered. "He'd delegate that bit of nastiness to someone else."

"But who would dare?" Miranda mused.

Ileana didn't hear her. Her stomach twisted, and she felt suddenly, overwhelmingly woozy. It was a feeling both familiar and distant, welcome but startling. It hadn't happened to her for a while . . . not since the shocking moment she'd found out that Thantos was her father.

Now her eyes glazed over, everything went blurry — then, like an auto-focus camera, the scene in front of her was sharp, defined. Ileana saw a girl standing on a cliff above a wildly tossing sea. In her hands she clutched an open book, its pages ruffled by the wind. The girl's black cape billowed in the gust, as did her long raven hair. She had violet eyes and a slash of scarlet lipstick lit her smug lips as she read the pages of Karsh's journal.

Miranda had no such vision. Instead, the older witch suddenly knew something the younger did not. As if it had been whispered in her ear, she heard the name:

Sersee.

CHAPTER FIVE
SENSITIVES AND PROTECTORS

It was late spring and easy to see it, Cam thought, sitting at the top of the soccer field bleachers behind Marble Bay High. How could she not have noticed the profusion of daffodils, the vivid new greenness of the bushes and bursting tree buds?

And there was a green newness in her, too. Saturday night, for the first time, she'd been able to hear the thoughts of someone other than Alex. But whose thoughts were they? Who had known, as she and Alex had, that something bad was about to happen?

Cam drew her arm across her forehead, swabbing

soccer sweat with the sleeve of her team sweatshirt. Practice was over for the day, and she needed a couple of minutes alone, some downtime to replay what had happened at the premiere.

The image of the robed lunatic haunted her. Some crazed weirdo had shown up way too close for comfort, just miles from Marble Bay, her safe haven. Was that past tense now?

She wanted to go over what she knew about the Witch Hunter — everything about him. The near-miss car crash, his psycho ranting at Brice, and his last menacing words to them, "You're next. All three of you." Who was this guy, and what did he want with them?

A breeze ruffled the strands of auburn hair that had escaped her scrunchied ponytail. It was a warm breeze, but it chilled her. As did the uninvited memory it seemed to have carried.

Out of nowhere, Cam remembered the cave on Coventry Island. Lit by blazing candles, its stony walls were slick and icy. There was a chain attached to one of its dank walls, a chain that held a sick, pacing panther. The groaning beast had once been . . . Jason.

"You okay?"

Cam opened her eyes and there he was. Jason Weissman. Tall, athletic, grinning with the brash joy that always lit his face when he saw her. Jason, her honey and wanna-be hero, her best guy pal, the kind and gentle boy Sersee had turned into a wounded beast.

Sersee. Cam couldn't rid herself of the bitter memory: ebony hair and a pale, contemptuous face that held mocking violet eyes. Ambitious, jealous, reckless, and skilled in the craft far beyond her years, the wicked young witch abused her formidable powers, destroying all and anything in her way, casting painful curses and vicious spells to get what she wanted.

With the help of Ileana and Miranda, Cam and Alex had been able to reverse Sersee's spells and erase the entire Sersee episode from Jason's mind. If only, Cam thought, she could erase it from her own . . .

"Cami, hey, wait till you hear this." Jason thumped down next to her, his buff, six-foot-two bulk bouncing the bench.

Cam blinked at him, blinked herself back to the moment. Realizing, as she did, how glad she was to see him. It felt good to know that whatever happened — no matter that a witch-hating, witch-hunting maniac was on the loose — Jason would have her back. He was dependable, heroic, daring. Hadn't he followed her all the way to Coventry just to protect her?

"Hey!" Jason was psyched. "Don't you want to hear my big news?"

"Definitely." Cam forced a smile — then seeing, really *seeing,* his flushed and classic face, realized she meant it. "What are you so hyped about?"

"I made the team. First string. I'm gonna play for Nebraska next season. I mean, I've got a real shot at it. That's what they're saying. They called yesterday —"

"Excellent!"

Jase was a basketball prodigy. For the game, his height was only adequate but his skill with the ball was awesome. It had won him a fat sports scholarship.

"Yeah," Jason continued, "I'm splitting right after graduation. I'm at training camp for the summer."

His excitement was contagious. "That's fabulous!" Cam affirmed. "Oh, Jase, that's wonderful. That'll be —" And then she stopped. And looked at him. And swallowed hard. "Oh, no. You're leaving." The words escaped before she could bite them back.

"Yeah, but after graduation," he reminded her, his expression suddenly unsure. "We've still got a couple of weeks till then. Cami . . ." he said cautiously, "I've gotta go. Okay? I just wanted you to be the first to know —"

"Sure. Um . . ." Why was she feeling so blue? So . . . "abandoned"? This was a good thing times two, she tried to tell herself. Jason would realize his dream and, as a bonus, stay safe. Win-win. The farther he was from her, the better off he'd be. Right? No one would use him as bait to get at her and Alex; no one would capture him or cast spells or try to morph him into some evil carnivorous creature.

But she'd miss him. A lot.

Snap out of it, she told herself. It's not like you're going to be alone this summer. And if your back needs covering, there's always Ileana, Miranda . . . Alex.

Determined to pump up her deflated heart, Cam took a deep breath and managed to smile — brightly, she hoped. "Jase, it's wonderful. No kidding. I'm totally psyched for you —"

"So we're cool?" Relieved, he planted an enthusiastic kiss on her cheek and took off.

Alex, heading toward the bleachers, almost bumped into him in her eagerness to get to her twin. They laughed, Jason and she. "Where's the fire?" he asked.

"In my heart," Alex quipped, hurrying past him.

"Yo, Cami — wait till you hear what's up," Alex said.

"You've discovered the true identity of the Witch Hunter," her sister said with a weird combo of sadness and sarcasm.

"That's on tomorrow's To Do list." Alex would not be put off. "Remember Cade?"

Cade Richman. Alex's tall, dark, and handsome crushee of last year. How could Cam forget? Cade, the boy who'd come closest to melting that lump of spiked concrete that Alex called her heart. Cade, who had lived in a mansion in Marble Bay Heights but came to school in skinny jeans, black tees, and biker boots. Those boots were made for walkin', Cam thought, remembering Alex's angst when Cade and his family moved to Paris at the end of the school year.

"He's coming back. I picked up my e-mail in computer lab five minutes ago and there was this excellent letter from him saying he was going to be in Marble Bay this summer!"

Cam couldn't speak. She could hardly breathe. She twisted her mouth into a jerk-o-lantern grin and just blinked at her ecstatic sister. For the second time in ten minutes, she was being called upon to act happy when she felt crappy. Not that she begrudged Alex a summer fling. It was just that . . .

"What?!" Alex demanded, having read Cam's thoughts. "You think I'm going to put Cade ahead of the deranged sucker who threatened our lives? No way, Camay. As far as I'm concerned, it just pushes up the deadline."

"What deadline?" Cam asked.

"The deadline for catching and crushing the costumed creep."

But at dinner, while Cam pushed food around on her plate and obsessed about the Witch Hunter, Alex was all Cade this and Cade that. And when it was time to do the dishes, she begged unashamedly to be allowed to check her computer for messages and promised she'd do more than her share the next day.

When Emily, Cam's adoptive mom, started to object, Dave signaled her with a tiny shake of his curly head to let Alex go.

"I'm on garbage detail. You don't need me till later, right?" Dylan, Cam's brother and Emily and Dave's bio-son, reminded them, scrambling after Alex.

"Em, we can handle this." Dave pushed back from the table and began to collect the dinner dishes. "Why don't you relax tonight?"

Emily gratefully acquiesced. "Holler if you two need any help," she offered, happily heading for the den.

"It's okay. I don't need help," Cam told her dad.

"No, no, no. It's all right," Dave insisted. "I'd like to . . . Consider it quality family time."

Cam eyed him suspiciously. You could practically monitor Dave's feelings by the weathervane of his bushy mustache. A congenitally happy soul, his whiskers usually tilted upward. When he was upset, he tugged them down, sometimes mindlessly chewing on an end. Right now, they were centered but tending downward, signaling a thoughtful mood. Or one of perplexed concern.

Cam put the platter she was carrying into the sink. "Okay, what's up?" she said.

"Good question, I was about to ask you the same thing."

"Noth —" she began automatically.

"And don't say 'nothing,'" Dave plowed on. "I can feel it, sense it. You're upset about something. Is it about that nut who crashed the premiere Saturday night? Or because Jason's leaving early for college?"

Alex had volunteered that info the moment they sat down to dinner.

"No." Cam did denial at first, then changed it to "Sort of. A little of both, I guess. Dad —" She had an idea. "When you say you can sense it, you know, 'feel' that something's wrong, what do you mean? Do you mean like a regular person? Or do you still have that . . . 'mojo' Karsh spotted in you?"

"Karsh." Dave sat back down at the table and waved for Cam to join him. "Is that what's going on? You miss him, don't you? You and Alex haven't been the same since you came back from his funeral, from Coventry."

Dave alone in Cam's mainland family knew of their visit to their island birthplace. He alone knew — had known — the beloved old warlock who had saved their lives as infants. Karsh himself had chosen Dave to be Cam's protector.

"Did anything happen there that you didn't tell me?" Dave asked now. "Something troubling?"

"Why?" Cam challenged. "What do you feel? Can you see things that aren't here and now? Can you hear what I'm thinking?"

Dave's mustache flagged. Then he understood what his child was asking and it returned to its normal optimistic upswing. "Okay, let's talk," he agreed.

Gratefully, Cam sat down across from him.

"When I first met Karsh, I was getting pretty good at knowing — knowing, sensing, not actually hearing," he clarified, "what people thought. I was . . . highly intuitive, I guess. Karsh called me a Sensitive. Of course, when I showed him what I could do, which was embarrassingly amateurish, very basic — I mean I could make assumptions about people based on . . . feelings I got about them, vibes — Karsh laughed.

"You remember that laugh of his?" Dave asked his daughter. "Never mocking. Always with you, not at you, always on your side. I met him at a paranormal conference, you know, a sort of convention of geeks interested in extrasensory perception, psychic healing, using one's mind to accomplish amazing feats — things most people think of either as magic or madness —"

"And you got to talking . . ." Cam knew the story

and tried to move Dave along. "And he really liked you and thought you'd make a perfect dad —"

"A perfect *Protector*," Dave corrected her. "A Protector is a person of high intuition and intelligence — hey, I'm quoting Karsh here," he added modestly. "A Sensitive with a strongly developed capacity for loyalty, love, and support. Being called Dad is all gravy. As for perfect, there's no such animal, honey. Protectors, like everyone else in the world, are human and, therefore, flawed. In fact, before I agreed to take you, Karsh told me stories about failed Protectors. People who were given fledgling witches and warlocks to rear but couldn't handle it. Either because they were too weak or their charges were too strong."

This was a piece of the story — a dark, chilling part — Cam hadn't heard before. "But you wanted to be a Protector, anyway?"

"It wasn't that so much. . . . That first meeting with Karsh happened a couple of years before your mom and I got married. We met again, at another conference, some years later. By then Emily and I had tried and failed to have a child of our own. Of course I mentioned it to him. There was nothing I couldn't talk to him about. I don't remember anything else about that meeting. Except . . ." Dave seemed to recall it now. "I think he asked whether I'd be willing to forgo, to give up or lose my own growing abilities in order to nurture another person's — a being whose potential far outshone my own, possibly a child's.

"I said I thought so. I mean, I was just dabbling. I was using telekinesis and ESP as party tricks to entertain friends. Karsh seemed to be asking whether I'd trade that in to help someone who'd use his or her skills for more important reasons. To do good things, to help others. To help, I think he said, the universe and everything in it. Something like that. It wasn't until he brought you to me," Dave said, reaching across the table and gently taking Cam's hand, "that he spoke of warlocks and witches. But by then it was too late. I'd taken one look at you and knew, instantly, there was no turning back."

Alex heard, though she'd tried not to, the conversation between Dave and Cam. It made her feel empty at first, whistled through her like a cold wind. These were the times she felt most alone. The Barnes family had taken her in, done everything they could to make her feel included — but there was no way she'd ever be as connected to Dave and Emily as Cam was.

She'd had her own Protector, Sara Fielding. She wondered now whether Sara also had given up her witchy gifts to take care of her. And . . . if she'd kept them, would she have been able to save herself? Could she have cheated death, beaten cancer, somehow gotten better . . . ?

Alex wished she'd had more time with her mother. Correction, as Cam would say: with her *Protector*. With Sara. She wished she could ask, like Cam just had, what Sara's life had been like before she'd met Karsh — how he'd found her and why he'd chosen her.

Most of all, Alex wanted to know whether she herself could have cast a spell, used herbs and crystals, willed the cancer cells to leave Sara's ravaged lungs the way she'd willed the weapon to leave the Witch Hunter's hand.

"So, where is he?" Dylan's voice punctured her ballooning sadness.

"What?" She spun on the desk chair, turning away from the computer to face him. Had Dylan, Emily and Dave's only bio-child, just read her mind? For a stunning moment Alex stared at Cam's blond brother, blinking in wonder.

"The French connection." Dylan hit a chord on his guitar. "The Paris . . . defection." He strummed again. "Cade's, um, direction —"

Cade! He meant Cade. Of course. She'd been about to check her e-mail when her head got all into the downstairs dialogue between Cam and Dave.

Alex relaxed, laughed. "Yo, Mr. Sass. You may be from Mass," she shot back at Dylan, "but give it up, bro. You ain't no Thoreau."

"Word up, woman," Dylan responded, grinning wide. "So what's Cade say? When's he getting here? Like, where is he now?"

"In England," Alex answered, as Dylan moseyed over casually and checked out her computer screen. She didn't add: "I think." Because it was more than that. . . .

Cade was in England. In London, to be exact. In a hotel room . . .

Alex *sensed* it. Knew it.

It was as if Dylan's question had flipped a switch. The moment she tried to answer it, this totally weird thing had happened behind her eyelids. Continents had scrawled by in a blur. Anonymous places and people. Their noise, at first a jumble of sounds, languages, and accents, slowed. Then the scrawling, which had been accompanied by a rising ticking noise, suddenly stopped. She couldn't see anything. She just knew.

"He's on his way," she told Dylan, both shocked and excited.

It was Dylan's turn to blink. "You didn't open your e-mail yet. How do you know that?"

Alex looked at the screen. Dyl was right. The screen saver was still on.

She took a breath, sucking air for time. "'Cause I'm a witch," she teased.

He frowned at her, not liking or buying the answer.

"It was in his last e-mail," she lied.

"Better watch out, witchy sistah, the Witch Hunter's gonna get ya." Dylan struck another chord, then set down his guitar. "If you're so witchy-girl cool, why don't you track that maniac who attacked Brice Stanley the other night?"

Lightbulb. Track. The word popped out of Dyl's sarcastic challenge. Tracker, Alex thought. Dave was talking about Sensitives and Protectors. But Karsh had been a tracker. The highest level a warlock or witch could attain.

Another word came to her. This one Dylan hadn't spoken. Didn't know.

Artemis. It was her birth name. What she'd been called as an infant, what she was known as on Coventry.

She'd read about Artemis in mythology books. Artemis, the huntress. Twin of Apollo, the sun god.

Surely, one of a huntress's skills was tracking.

Now she remembered. At the premiere. She'd known the Witch Hunter had slipped away from them.

She'd seen his dark car doing 80, taking a corner at mach speed, escaping —

She'd known where he was then. Could she find him now? Could she locate him the way she'd just located Cade? Could she harness this unpredictable new power budding inside her? Could she track and nail the Witch Hunter?

CHAPTER SIX
FEAR BITES

At lunch, the twins usually sat at different tables. Cam hung with her Six Pack squad; Alex ate with Dylan and the slacker-boarder-rapper crew. They were halfway through lunch when the message came.

Cam got it garbled, muffled, nothing but a menacing murmur.

She quickly looked over at Alex — before the migraine came. Her head got suddenly heavy, as it did when she felt a vision coming on, but she could still focus. What she saw was her sister glaring around the cafeteria, trying to find the culprit who had just threatened them.

What did you hear? Cam desperately telegraphed Alex.

Hold on. Wait, her twin sent back, her gray eyes still searching the funky premises. The art-class friendship and diversity murals, stainless steel steam tables, and wall of corporately sponsored soda and snack vending machines.

Cam decided to scope out the lunchroom, too. And saw nothing special. Just the usual suspects slouching in molded plastic chairs, chowing tray cuisine at neon-bright tables, their humongous backpacks at their heels. And the teachers, of course, laid back against the walls or cruising the aisles like prison trustees on a cushy assignment. And, alone at a table in the corner, the school's rarely spotted new maintenance man, Mr. Golem.

A commotion at her table called Cam's attention home. Bree was pushing away from the table, screeching, "Don't shpritz my cashmere!" Hand over her mouth, Kristen was cracking up. Beth was gathering napkins, trying to mop up the mess on the table. And Amanda was gently patting Sukari's back. The girl had choked on her soft drink and was coughing and spraying carbonated slush from her nose.

Cam's mind was becoming cloudy. Willing herself to stay alert, she turned back to Alex, a couple of tables away. *You did hear something, didn't you?* she asked again.

It was him. Her sister finally, silently spilled it. *Scythe sucker, the freak from the premiere.*

The Witch Hunter? Cam asked.

Or someone who shares his anti-us obsession.

"Oh, no, I think he saw you!"

For a moment, Cam thought the last line came from Alex. But it was Amanda. When Cam turned to her questioningly, Amanda laughed. "Sukari's crushed out on Mr. Spenser. All he has to do is glance her way and she can't remember which way is swallow and which way is spew."

Mr. Spenser was the AP science teacher. And Sukari was acing his advanced placement course.

"'Manda!" It was Sukari, somewhat recovered but still dabbing at her nose with a Beth-given napkin. "It has nothing to do with crushes. The guy is old enough to be my father. He's just . . . I don't know. Intense. I get nervous around him is all."

"He is kind of intense," Amanda said, eyeing the teacher in question . . . or rather, his back as he ambled out of the lunchroom.

"Well, he's no Brice Stanley." Bree had been bringing all convo back to the premiere since the gala event.

"Excuse me, can I talk to you for a minute?" Alex's sudden appearance at the Six Pack table and the impatient tone of her voice was an instant conversation killer.

"How'd you tear yourself away from slacker central?" Kristen ventured.

Alex silenced her with a look. "Camryn," she said.

Cam, for once, was happy to get away from the Six Pack dish. She got up and followed Alex over to the vending machines.

"Can you believe it?" Cam said. "He's here! The Witch Hunter is *in our school*."

And I heard him. I heard something, Cam thought, but wasn't sure.

Alex had read her mind — much more clearly than Cam had been able to read the Witch Hunter's.

"Did you also smell him? I did," Alex asserted, "and either his scent and sending range are awesome or he was somewhere around the cafeteria."

Shocked and trembling, Cam asked again, "What did he say?"

"He said," Alex answered, "'I see the three of you. I know who you are. I know *what* you are. And soon, everyone will know.'"

"The three of us?" Cam said. "Who is he talking about?"

"Yo," Alex shot back. "It's not just who he's talking about. It's who's doing the talking."

CHAPTER SEVEN
A DANGEROUS ALLIANCE

The girl had summoned him. Summoned Thantos DuBaer. Arrogant little guttersnipe, the hulking warlock thought, as he trudged beside the choppy waters of Lake Superior. Listening for her footsteps, he heard only the *whish* and *shush* of waves lapping Coventry's rocky shore.

He was in a hurry. Eager to leave the island and rush to the CompUMag plant in Massachusetts. How strange, he pondered, that there should have been a factory there all these years, a DuBaer-owned facility just miles from Marble Bay, where one of his nieces had lived for the past fifteen years and the other had come to more recently.

Had he spent more time at the CompUMag factory in Massachusetts this year, instead of his plants in Montana and California, he would have been within striking distance of the troublesome twins.

Well, he intended to make up for that oversight. As soon as the wretched little witch arrived to tell him what was so urgent.

Sersee Tremaine — he could not remember what her name had been when she arrived on the island. Or how old she had been. Eight, he thought, or nine at the most. She had come alone — angry, arrogant, a child who had turned against her Protector on the mainland and bragged about escaping from him.

How she had survived, Thantos couldn't imagine. But he knew that the wild young thing and her cohorts made their home in the woods and caves of Coventry. That she was said to be extremely skilled at the craft, had spied on enough ceremonies and initiation rites to have picked up powerful secrets and dangerous magic.

He knew all this because, not long ago, the girl had expressed interest in becoming one of his fledglings.

The lakeside wind pelted Thantos's cheeks, ripped through his dark curls and thick black beard. Expressed interest? The irritated warlock shook his head. That hardly described the campaign she had waged to capture his interest. And she had. The headstrong ragamuffin had intrigued him. But ultimately he had found her too rash and undisciplined, entirely too self-centered, to serve any master but her own bloated ego.

"Lord Thantos."

He looked up, annoyed at having to shield his eyes from stinging sunlight in order to search the cliff for her.

"I'm here." A slender figure in a flapping cape waved at him. "I'll be right down." Exasperated, he noted the trick. Through instinct or purpose, the arrogant little witch had found a way to snatch a trivial advantage, to have him blinded by sunlight, to literally stand above him. He had been right to be wary of her.

"I have a gift for you," she promised, as she scrambled, goat-sure, down the face of the cliff. "I'm glad you came. And you will be, too. It will be worth your . . . inconvenience."

Was she mocking him? Thantos searched the girl's eyes, purple as mountain asters. They were intentionally hooded. She had put up a screen to protect herself from inspection. Her thoughts, scrambled, closed to him, were as guarded as her gaze.

He could, of course, break through her safeguards. He was a tracker, after all. But the effort would be too time-and-energy consuming. Blast her. What was this . . . gift . . . that she had used to lure him?

"Why, it's right here, Lordship."

She was smiling coyly. Pleased to prove how adept she was at reading *his* thoughts. Thantos closed his mind to her — and reached for the book she had brought him.

"What is this?" he asked, noting the title — *Forgiveness or Vengeance*. But when he opened the book, he found, in its hollowed-out space, a sheaf of handwritten pages.

"The old warlock's last words," Sersee answered. "I think you'll find them interesting. I did. And surely Ileana must have. She is, after all," the little witch added, smiling insolently, "your *daughter*."

Thantos bit back the desire to immobilize the impudent urchin with a glare. He focused on the pages instead. And there they were, in Karsh's crabby scrawl, his father Nathaniel's words:

From this day forward, only women will decide the fate of the DuBaer dynasty. Tell my sons that none of them will rule, none will lead. I am the last patriarch. But they will provide leaders — their wives and daughters. . . .

"Fascinating, isn't it?"

"Quiet!" Thantos roared.

Sersee's slender shoulders hunched immediately. She spun away, covering her face with the hem of her billowing cape as if expecting the powerful tracker to try to catch her eye, to call up a spell that would silence her permanently. Or worse.

"Why did you bring me this . . . this senile old warlock's fantasy?! What did you expect to gain?"

The cape still covering her face, Sersee's voice was muffled. "Only your . . . regard, Lordship. I wished only to prove my worth to you."

"You want my regard, yet you cower before me, you don't trust me," Thantos shouted at her.

Sersee turned cautiously. Warily, she let down her cape. Still more guardedly, she looked directly at the mighty tracker.

Thantos smiled. And stared into the young witch's remarkable violet eyes. And with a wave of his hand, paralyzed her.

CHAPTER EIGHT
GOING UNDERGROUND

"Can't sleep?" Cam asked. She didn't look over at Alex's bed. She didn't have to. Even if the full moon outside their window hadn't lit their room like a 100-watt bulb, her twin had been grunting and shifting and muttering for what seemed like an hour.

"Understatement alert," Alex answered, mimicking one of the Six Pack's favorite sayings. "Is it Mr. Golem in the basement with a hood or Mrs. Hammond's secretary in the principal's office with a detention slip?"

"You're obsessing about the Witch Hunter?" Cam sat up.

"Same as you," Alex snapped back, kicking off the covers and sitting up, too. Having read her twin's mind, she added, "Why? Did you think Cade was my only obsession?"

"Guilty." They faced each other in the moonlit room. "At lunch. He said three again, Als."

"I'm the one who heard him," her sister reminded her. "Three. That's you, me, and someone else. Let's do the math. The Witch Hunter said 'three of you' at the premiere, and 'three of you' in the cafeteria. Who's been with us both times?"

"The Six Pack?!" Cam said incredulously.

"That's right," Alex answered. "One of your crew — who, as far as I can tell, are exceptional only in how boringly ordinary they are. Can you imagine Beth casting spells or Bree having a premonition about anything other than when shoes go on sale at The Bootery?"

"This is insane," Cam said. "Are you really saying that one of my friends is a *witch*?"

Alex thought for a second. "Well, the Witch Hunter got us and Brice right. So obviously he knows something we don't."

That shut Cam up. "How about Amanda?" she finally asked. "She's always been totally open to mystical possibilities —"

"And you know that because she wears sandals, toe rings, and Indian print skirts?"

"That's not fair," Cam protested. "'Manda's extremely empathetic. She's deeply intuitive about other people's pain and distress —"

"So is the pet psychic," Alex pointed out.

"Are you through?"

"And she does it without crystals, candles, and incense," her sister added. "Okay. Now I'm through."

"Sukari's out of the question. She's a rabid realist, a skeptical show-me girl," Cam announced, beginning to feel sleepy. "That leaves . . . Kristen? Could she be a witch?" she asked doubtfully.

Alex shook her head. "Only if it would impress Bree. Cam —" She turned serious. "How could he know about us unless he's a witch — or a warlock — himself? And if he is, why is he on this rampage against, you know, his own kind?"

Cam had been mulling that over. Her talk with Dave had reminded her of what Brice Stanley had said about the man — that he probably had some advanced degree of intuition or ESP. . . .

Alex picked up on her twin's thoughts immediately. "You're saying he's not a dues-paying, initiated member of the witches union?"

"I didn't *say* anything," Cam reminded her, annoyed. "If you'd use your mind for something other than eavesdropping on mine, you might come up with some other possibility."

"Why bother?" Alex was too intrigued to argue. "Come on, spill. If he isn't a warlock or a full-fledged fledgling, then what? You think he's a Sensitive?"

"A Sensitive or —" What had Dave called it? Cam stretched drowsily. "A failed Protector. Someone who was supposed to support and take care of a young witch or warlock but hadn't or couldn't."

"A failed Protector?" Alex shivered, which let her know that Cam, with Dave's help, was onto something. "I'll tell you what I can't stand," she announced. "In addition to not knowing who or what this guy is, I can't stand not knowing *where* he is! The whole idea that he's creeping around the school, hanging out in the lunchroom —"

"Als, did you see Mr. Golem, you know, the maintenance guy or whatever? There's something creepy about him. Did you see him in the lunchroom today?"

Alex leaned forward expectantly. "Why? Did you get a vibe from him?"

Cam shrugged and fell back onto her bed. "No," she said, snuggling back under her soft summer blanket. "No vibe. Nothing. It was just a thought."

"How 'bout tomorrow we sneak down to Mr.

Golem's office in the basement and scope it out," Alex suggested.

It was lunchtime. There'd been a Golem sighting in the cafeteria again — complete with Bree pointing and whispering, "Yeuw, he reminds me of the nutcase at the premiere." And Beth's blasé response, "*Everything* reminds you of the premiere."

With less than twenty minutes before classes began again, and who knew how long before Golem himself decided to return to his den in the bowels of Marble Bay High, the twins jumped at the op to check out the maintenance man's home base.

Knowing they had to work quickly, they crept down the fire stairs, Cam noting the big ax hanging next to the foam canister on the first landing, Alex sniffing the cool, dank air hoping to pick up the putrid scent of the Witch Hunter.

The school basement was a maze of rooms. But only one door had a hand-lettered sign on it that read KEEP OUT. That was the one Alex pushed open after a quick nod from Cam.

Golem's habitat reminded Alex of a cave. And since the most memorable cave she'd ever been in was the one on Coventry Island where she, Cam, and Jason had been held captive, the place gave her the heebie-jeebies.

Cam, whom Alex would have bet would be even more spooked poking around the school's subterranean depths, seemed oblivious to the fact that they were underground.

To be fair, Golem's domain was much nicer and totally better kept than the dungeon where Sersee and her pals played.

There was nothing visibly strange on the maintenance man's desk or on the thick wooden table above which his tools were neatly arrayed.

Using one of his ladders, Alex checked out the tops of what seemed like miles of insulated pipe hanging from his workshop ceiling. Cam helped herself to gloves from a box of carefully matched pairs and snooped under, around, and over discarded water heaters, old circuit breaker boxes, and what looked like an enormous cold and rusty furnace.

All the while, the twins agreed, there was no real juice in the place, no heat, no telltale vibe that sent shivers down their spines or raised hackles on the backs of their necks.

They had only a few minutes left. While Cam went through the contents of a metal file cabinet, Alex examined an old wooden cupboard filled with folded rags, cans of turpentine, brushes of every size, and gallons of the puke-green paint that covered the basement walls.

And there was a pint of brilliant red paint, too, sitting in a small, spilled puddle — which Alex discovered was wet when she stupidly tested it with her fingertips.

Through the pale fumes of paint and turpentine, the rotten-egg smell came to her. And then her hyper hearing picked up a door creaking at the top of the stairwell and Mr. Golem's shuffling tread.

The next thing she knew, Cam had seized her hand and pulled her out of the workshop. In the basement corridor, they faced a warren of doors, almost all padlocked. Twirling helplessly, trying to find a place to hide, Cam spotted one that was open a crack.

They charged through the door a second before Golem reached the landing.

The room was pitch-black. The windows had been painted over. And the toxic-dump stench was stronger here than in the maintenance man's headquarters. The smell was more about the Witch Hunter than the unwashed dampness of a cellar.

"What can you see?" Alex asked, trusting Cam's supersight to scope out the tiny room they'd escaped into.

"I think we're in . . . like, a broom closet," Cam ventured. "I mean, I don't see any actual brooms, but there are . . . shovels and . . . crowbars, I think. And, like, random tools lying around."

"But what smells?" Alex pressed. "Are there rags

around or, like, a stinky mop? Something — anything — odor could cling to?"

Cam looked around, sniffed the fetid air of the closet, but couldn't smell what Alex did.

"Over there. In that corner." Taking her twin by the shoulders, Alex turned her toward the place the stench was strongest. "Can you see anything in that corner?"

"Yes!" Cam yipped. "There's a bag on the floor. A big canvas bag, almost like a duffel, but with brown leather trim and handles —"

A blinding light lit the dark room. Cam put her hands over her eyes. Alex winced at the electric brilliance. Suddenly, their hiding place was bright as day.

"What are you doing in here?!" Mr. Golem demanded, a giant searchlight in his hand. He seemed as startled to see them as they were to see him. "You kids are not allowed down here. No kids allowed. You could get hurt. Or worse." He spotted the red paint on Alex's hand and became wildly agitated. "You were messing with my things, weren't you?! You should never have come down here —"

They didn't apologize; they didn't even bother to make up an excuse. The adrenaline pumping in their chests suddenly hit their feet and they bolted, half expecting to feel Golem's thick hands trying to hold them back.

CHAPTER NINE
SERSEE ON THE ROCKS

They knew who had taken Karsh's journal — the treacherous and talented young witch who had tried to destroy the twins. Now she had stolen their birthright, the only proof beyond doubt of what was rightfully theirs.

As they made their way toward the shore where Ileana had seen the girl in her vision, Ileana and Miranda were torn by warring feelings. Their minds knew their mission: to track the thief and get back the book. But their emotions flashed between anger and excitement.

The anger was reserved for the dangerous urchin, Sersee.

The waves of excitement that shot through them

were for the miracle of their returned powers. Precious skills they'd thought were lost forever had returned — maybe only a few, maybe only for a moment, but something wonderful had happened. Ileana had had a vision; Miranda had known the culprit's name.

What remained to be revealed was why the criminal, cave-dwelling imp had chosen, among all of Ileana's precious things, a book? That book! Of what value could Karsh's revelations be to such a single-minded, self-serving child?

"Look there, up ahead." Miranda pointed to the girl. Ahead of them, standing at the crest of a sea-battered cliff, Sersee stood still as stone. Her black hair tangled and twirled like seaweed battered by tides. Her violet cape flared and flapped wildly in the wind. She looked much as she had in Ileana's vision — but not exactly the same. For one thing, the book was gone. For another, the girl, who would certainly have heard them coming, hadn't even turned her head to look at them. She stood too still.

"Something's wrong," Ileana said, her voice falling to a whisper.

"Has she been . . . transformed? Put under a spell?" Miranda asked cautiously.

You call yourselves witches?

Ileana and Miranda both picked up the sarcastic, unspoken grumble. It was coming, naturally, from the frozen girl.

Duh. Of course I've been transformed. And if one of you passing geniuses doesn't undo the spell, I'll be a pillar of salt by morning —

Ileana approached the motionless young witch. Clasping her hands behind her back, she slowly began to circle Sersee. "My, oh my, what a sad predicament," she mused, her lips barely holding back a grin.

Miranda drew near. "She's paralyzed," she said, sounding disgustingly sincere to Ileana. "How awful. Ileana, we must do something."

Yes. You must. Sersee sent the angry, urgent message. *It is your duty as witches to heal, to help —*

"Oh, it is, it is," Ileana agreed. "However, I, for one, see no reason to hurry. Particularly since you can tell us now — before we warm your blood and ignite your senses again — why you broke into my cottage, why you stole —"

Never, Sersee swore.

Ileana bristled and might even have struck the insolent little witch had Miranda not laid a hand on her arm. "Don't. Please," she urged. "The child has been through enough."

What? Sersee was as surprised as Ileana by Miranda's

intervention. *How do you know?* she snapped defensively. *You, a DuBaer, who lives in luxury at Crailmore, an initiated "Lady," accepted and respected by all?*

"We would like to help you," Miranda assured her a bit brusquely. "Were we not on such an urgent mission ourselves, we would gladly free you from this wretched condition —"

"Are you crazy?!" Ileana sputtered. "Free her? Why I'd sooner laminate her —"

Suddenly, the cliff was alive with shadows. Ileana felt them, then saw a fire. In the midst of black smoke and leaping flames, a man stood with his fist raised, shouting curses. In a heap at his feet was a woman with flowing black hair. She clutched his legs, begging for the life of her child. Suddenly, Ileana was overwhelmed by waves of despair and pity. She saw an infant crawling through the woods, her tattered clothes singed and still smoking.

The tiny child, she knew, was Sersee.

Stunned, she turned to Miranda. The twins' remarkable mother seemed to have had no vision, no unasked-for trip down the evil urchin's memory lane. Did she know the girl's history or was she merely being Miranda, blindly kind and trusting?

As if the placid witch had heard her, Ileana noticed for the first time a glint in Miranda's metallic eyes.

"But before we come to your aid," Miranda was telling Sersee, "we must find Lord Karsh's journal. If only you knew where it was; if only you could help us —"

Ninnies! Of course I know where it is. Only release me from this heinous state and I'll tell you everything! Right now! This stinking, wretched wind is killing my complexion. And don't even ask what it's doing to my hair!

"No fear," Miranda assured the girl, as Ileana's head commenced to pound. "I have herbs aplenty to soothe your beautiful skin and revitalize your raven hair. Only tell me, child, while Ileana prepares her un-morphing spell, where is the journal now?"

Ileana eyed Miranda with bleary admiration. The wily woman was playing Sersee! She had lapsed into good cop/bad cop without blinking an eye. While Ileana had stood there holding the vinegar jar, Miranda was luring Sersee with honey.

But what had she just said? While Ileana prepares her un-morphing spell? Right. An uninvited vision was one thing, but just how, Ileana wanted to know, was she supposed to make magick, activate the frozen brat all on her own? Did wily Miranda even want her to break the spell? Together, she and Miranda had taught the spell to Cam and Alex; together, she and Miranda had discovered who had stolen the journal and where the guilty party was.

That was it! Ileana's gray eyes widened in wonder. That was the key, the secret. Together. Just as Cam's and Alex's abilities increased when they were together, so had her wilted powers blossomed anew in Miranda's presence.

Your precious book is on its way to the mainland, Sersee told them, *in the hands of the most disloyal, deceitful, double-crossing warlock Coventry has ever seen, the same treacherous tracker who cast this spell on me. Three guesses. Could it be Thantos DuBaer, Thantos DuBaer, or Thantos DuBaer? Buzzzz, your time is up. The answer is . . . the ungrateful, underhanded Thantos DuBaer!*

Miranda gasped involuntarily.

Told you so, Ileana couldn't help thinking.

Hello! I'm waiting, Sersee's snotty inner voice insisted.

Miranda glanced at Ileana. "We are honor-bound," she said. "I gave my word and we must do as I promised." But she looked distraught, deflated suddenly. And Ileana realized it was not because Thantos had possession of the book. Perhaps he meant to return it, naive Miranda mused. No, it was the sudden knowledge that he had done this, paralyzed a wayward child, which revolted Miranda.

Ileana took her hand. "I have crystals and herbs in my pouch," she told Miranda. "Why don't you begin the incantation while I arrange them?"

"Do you think we can?" Miranda asked, distracted.

Sersee heard her and freaked. *Oh, no.* The trapped girl's panicked thoughts came through to them. *Please don't tell me that you two are as "DuBaer" as the Hulk? You're not going to un-morph me, are you? You're going to leave me like this. Don't get me wrong, when I said deceitful and underhanded, I meant it with total respect.*

The ceremony, the spell-casting, exhausted Miranda and Ileana.

At its end, they stood over Sersee, who had collapsed and lay in a heap at their feet — a heap that reminded the weary Ileana of the woman in her vision.

But Sersee was not pleading. Her body had simply forgotten its purpose. It would take a minute or two before the collapsed girl could move properly again.

Seeing her this way, vulnerable and breathing hard like a cornered animal, struck a chord in Miranda. "I remember you," she said, surprising herself and Ileana. "It was shortly before Aron was killed. You were —"

"An orphan," Sersee broke in. "I was . . . on my own."

"Yes, it was terrible. We had all seen the smoking ruins and believed that you'd perished with your parents. You were so tiny, so bright, so alone —"

"You might say nothing much has changed," the young witch pointed out.

CHAPTER TEN
MENACING MESSAGES

Cam's knees grew weak. The writing was on the wall. Literally. There, on the side of the school that faced the soccer field, was a message painted in red. IT'S EASY TO WIN WITH WITCHCRAFT.

"Golem!" Cam whispered to Alex, who had walked onto the field with her. "He's got to be the Witch Hunter."

"You had a vision?" Alex asked, surprised.

"No," Cam confessed. "It's just the paint —"

"Something tells me not," Alex whispered quickly, as Bree, Kristen, and Beth trotted onto the field behind them, suited up for practice.

Kristen was first among Cam's teammates to notice the sign. "Cool," she said, "or it would be if we were the Wildcats." The Salem Wildcats were the Marble Bay Meteors' arch soccer rivals.

Beth inspected the red painted message. "What's that supposed to mean? What's going on around here?"

Cam seized on Kristen's comment. "It's probably some lame Salem joke to rattle us before the semis. You know — Salem, witchcraft, that kind of thing. Where are 'Manda and Suke?" she asked, hoping to divert her crew.

"Amanda's got a dental, and Sukari's got a mental," Bree quipped.

"Which means?" Beth wanted to know.

"Which means," Bree's shadow, Kristen, piped up, "that Amanda is at Dr. No Pain, No Gain, and Sukari's doing extra-credit work in Dr. Frankenstein's chem lab."

Cam's nostrils twitched involuntarily. *Chem lab,* she found herself thinking.

The coach's whistle put an end to her guesswork. Cam hurried onto the field with the rest of the Meteors. Alex had planned to hurry home to check her computer for news on Cade's whereabouts. But once more, suddenly, she knew!

Her tracking system revved into action again. A

whoosh of wind seemed to blow past her ears. Cade was in London, it said. And then a second, louder rush of air carried the news that he was at the airport. Cade was on his way! She knew it — as strangely and surely as she knew that Mr. Golem was not the Witch Hunter.

Sukari was crying. Cam and Alex ran into her in the girls' room after school. The minute she saw them, she blew her nose and put on this big phony smile. "Yo, wassup?" Suke tried for upbeat.

"Right back at you," Alex, no fan of subtlety, said. "Wassup yourself?"

The tall girl sighed deeply, her shoulders sagging.

Cam elbowed her sister out of the way. "Suke, are you okay?"

"Does she look okay?" Alex asked irritably. "That's mascara running down her face. You think she's trying to pass for a zebra?"

"It's Spenser," Sukari wailed. "He's, like, totally turned on me. He used to be all nice and encouraging, you know. I thought he liked me. But he's, like, all over my case now."

"About what?" Cam asked, wetting a tissue under a stream of sink water.

When Sukari hesitated, Alex intercepted her thought,

then silently blurted it out to her sister: *He wants to know how she gets all his quizzes right*.

Sukari glanced curiously at Alex. "He thinks I'm cheating or something," she said.

Cam squeezed the tissue and handed it to Suke. "He actually said that?"

Sukari looked from Alex to Cam and back again. *Don't make me say it,* Alex heard her plead.

Cam was waiting for an answer. "I mean, he didn't come right out and accuse you, did he?"

The bathroom door swung open. "Sukari!" It was Amanda, her tone, first annoyed, turned to concern. "I've been waiting for you outside. Suki, what's the matter? Are you crying? Oh, no. Don't let him get to you."

"Him?" Alex echoed. "Yo, Amanda, how do you know what we were talking about?"

"Excuse me?" The usually placid little redhead put her hands on her hips. "You know, for a Scorpio you're way overdefensive. I know what Suke's upset about because she's my bff and she tells me everything and even if she didn't, I have a sixth sense about these things. . . . And, anyway, it's been going on all semester."

"What has?" Cam jumped in.

"This push-pull thing she has with Spenser."

Amanda took the damp tissue from Sukari's hand and reached up with it to wipe the mascara spills off her best friend's cheeks. "One day he's wild for her — she's the best thing to happen to science since Madame Curie; the next, she's plotting to destroy the universe."

Sukari nodded. "He's been acting weird recently —" She stopped, hesitating.

Since the day after that dumb premiere, Alex heard her thinking. Or had it been Amanda's thoughts she'd picked up? Now she was totally confused.

"This place is a heinous hotbed of weirdos this year," Alex said, leading them on.

"You're right," Amanda picked up. "There's Spenser, the wild-eyed lab rat, Mr. I'm-all-rational-and-scientific. Except if you get perfect scores on his tests three times in a row he goes ballistic."

"Is that what happened with Suke?" Cam asked. But 'Manda was on a roll.

"And then there's Shenky in Mrs. Hammond's office. She's supposed to be school secretary, not hall-pass monitor." Amanda shook her head. "What an agenda. She nailed Bree three times last semester."

"And what about Golem?" Sukari wrinkled her nose. "There's something, like, so . . . *unsavory* about the man. He's . . . well, just plain sneaky."

"Golem." Cam looked pointedly at Alex, who shook her head.

"Or Spenser," Alex shot back.

"Or Shenky," Amanda piped up. "I mean, is this an institution of higher education or just an institution . . . like a zoo?"

CHAPTER ELEVEN
GROWTH SPURTS

"Als, something is happening," Cam announced that night when they were back in their room after dinner.

"Yo, give me news, not history," Alex grumbled, falling into the computer chair, which practically held her butt imprint since the day Cade had e-mailed that he was returning to Marble Bay.

"No, I mean, really. Something's changing . . . inside me."

"Hormones," Alex cracked dismissively.

"Alex. I can hear voices, voices other than yours, okay?!" Not normally one to give in to radical impulses, Cam seized the back of her sister's chair and spun Alex to face her. "I'm getting new abilities, new witchy skills —"

Red-faced with indignation, Alex was about to go off on her twin when, slowly, what Cam had said penetrated her Cade-crowded brain. She took a breath, crossed her arms, leaned back, and said, "Okay. You got my attention. Spill."

And Cam did. She told her sister, again, what Alex had refused to hear before — that ever since their return from Coventry Island, her senses, her extrasensory perception, her "mojo," had kicked up to a new level.

Before, only the eyes had it. Cam's intense gray eyes had been capable of seeing and searing. Now her hearing, even her sense of smell, she thought, had . . . well, *awakened*.

She didn't have Alex's abilities in those areas. She didn't have Alex's finely tuned ears and nose, her easy mind-reading skills or animal-sharp scenting. But lately, she'd heard sounds, muffled sentences, random words that she knew had sprung from the thoughts of people around her. And just this afternoon, Cam reported, when they were talking about Sukari in chem lab, something had tickled her nostrils. Not an actual smell, but the idea of a smell . . .

"Oh, forget it!" Cam threw herself across her bed. "I don't know what's going on or how to explain it, not even to you. It's like I'm having this weird psychic growth spurt. And, please, Alex, or Artemis, or whoever you are, spare me your sarcasm right now. It's bad enough I'm about to be outed by some freak at my school —"

"Oh, *you're* about to be outed?" Alex jumped in with two Doc Martens–wearing feet. "Like you're the only hot dog on the grill? Well, I'm right there, too, Ms. Oscar Meyer. For instance, my future-seeing powers may not be as hot as yours, but my On-Star is smokin'. Whatever is going down around here, Apolla, it isn't your solo show. It's you and me — and some poor third sucker — who are being haunted and taunted by said freak. Who, trust me, is not the antisocial maintenance man at *my* school."

"How would you know?" Cam demanded, sitting up, steaming. "And what was that crack about On-Star? You totally lost me —"

"If only," Alex shot back. "I'll show you how I know. Watch this." She whirled back to the computer console. "I haven't checked e-mail since this morning, when there was nothing from Cade online. So now, before I even glance at my messages, let me tell you that he is at Heathrow Airport in London, either about to board a plane or already on one. He is heading U.S.A.-ward this minute. And I know that because? Yo, I'm having a witchy little growth spurt of my own!"

Like a concert pianist, Alex let her poised hands fall, one on the keyboard, one on the mouse. She opened her e-mail screen, then scrolled through the messages. There it was, new mail from Cade.

She was about to click open his note, when Cam, who'd come up behind her to scan the screen, hollered, "Wait! What's that? Open that one!"

Subject: Your Time Has Come! Sender: WitchHunter1.

Alex glanced over her shoulder at Cam.

"Come on, hurry up. Open it," her sister urged, reaching for the mouse.

Alex swatted Cam's hand away and double-clicked. As she did, she again felt a noisy breeze blowing past her ears and cheeks. The spiky hair on her head didn't stir, but goose bumps prickled the nape of her neck as if a rasping wind had actually blown through the sturdy walls of their bedroom.

Cam's sudden whisper made things worse. "Als, I smell something . . . garlic and —"

"Rotten eggs," Alex confirmed. "Rotten eggs. Sulfur. Science lab . . ."

Cam felt sick. She grabbed the back of Alex's chair. "What does it say? Hurry!"

"Read it and weep," Alex growled angrily.

Cam blinked, trying to clear her sight, which had become blurry. Finally, she focused on the screen. And saw:

WITCHES, BE WARNED. YOU CANNOT HIDE IN MARBLE BAY. TOMORROW ALL WILL KNOW YOUR NAMES.

The message had not just been sent to Alex and Cam. They saw that it had gone out to every kid in the sophomore class.

"Tomorrow?" Cam grasped her throat as if choking on the deadline. "What can we do between today and tomorrow? It's seven o'clock, Als. We've got to find him now. Find him and stop him!"

Alex couldn't answer. She couldn't even think. Her head had begun pounding. She lowered it and closed her eyes. In the blackness, her sense of smell came even more vividly alive. The stench of burnt eggs, of stinging chemicals, clogged her nostrils. She swallowed and felt her stomach heave.

Moving blindly from desk to dresser to chair to wall, she made her way to the bathroom. There, she fell to her knees, resting her now-burning brow on the cold porcelain of the sink.

She must have lost consciousness. When she opened her eyes again and struggled to her feet, the sky outside the narrow bathroom window had turned the flaming pink of dusk. And when she lurched back into the bedroom she shared with Cam, her sister was gone.

Alex didn't have the strength to call out or go looking for her. She fell back on her own bed and waited for her balance, body, and mind to return.

CHAPTER TWELVE
THE HUNTER'S TALE

Cam couldn't wait. Okay, maybe Alex was right; maybe Mr. Golem wasn't the Witch Hunter, but the answer, Cam was convinced, was at the school. It was either someone who worked there, or someone who could sneak in.

As she approached Marble Bay High, she saw two cars pull out of the staff parking lot. One she recognized as Principal Hammond's, the other was being driven by Golem.

Cam turned away quickly, bent down, and pretended to be tying her sneaker. She was pretty sure he hadn't seen her. Golem was her strongest suspect — should she follow him? How, on foot? She shook her head, trying to clear it of idiotic ideas. It was better that he was gone, she decided. She waited until his car disappeared from view. It was nondescript, old, and dark, but something told her it wasn't the one that had nearly rammed the limo.

Relieved, she scrambled to her feet and checked the lot again.

Only three vehicles were left. Two she recognized: the beat-up station wagon in which Mr. Hadley, the basketball coach, hauled sports equipment, and the red VW with the vanity plate 123 ED, which everyone called the "math-mobile" because it belonged to Eletha Denadio, who taught advanced calculus. Cam couldn't immediately ID the third car.

A blast of sweat erupted on her forehead a second before she realized that it was — or might have been — the dark car driven by the Witch Hunter the night of the premiere. Parked in the staff parking lot.

Against the urge that said "run," she headed toward the parked car. Its glass was tinted but, with her hand hooding her eyes, Cam stuck her face against the front window. On the seat was an ordinary leather briefcase, a stack of blue test booklets, and a striped scarf.

Well, what had she expected to see, a photo ID driver's license?

The sun was falling fast. Already the trees surrounding the school were casting long-fingered shadows. Cam rubbed the nose smudge she'd left on the windshield with her sweatshirt sleeve and hurried toward the soccer field. Like many of the Meteors, she had a key to the gym door for after-practice lockup. She used it now, wondering if she'd run into the girls' coach or anyone else who might have lingered behind to use the sports center.

Her sneakers squeaked as she hurried across the polished basketball court. She thought about Jason, almost sniffed the dead air in the locked gym as if expecting to catch a whiff of his soapy neck, his clean, dark curls. The thought of him warmed her, made her smile, but only until the memory that he'd soon be leaving caught up. She was out in the hall, blindsided by self-pity, when a door at the end of the corridor slammed and she froze in fear.

They'll be here soon, she heard a voice say. *One final check*. And then she realized that no one had spoken aloud. She had read someone's mind. Not Alex's. Not one of the "witchy" members of the Six Pack. His mind. The Witch Hunter's.

Determined footsteps echoed in the near-empty corridor. Cam flattened herself against the tiled wall, hiding as best she could at the end of a bank of lockers. Her heart seemed to have leaped into her ears, thudding deafeningly, blocking out all other noise. By the time it quieted, the footsteps and the sound of his thinking were gone.

She hurried through the fire door leading to the basement. Mr. Golem's office and work area were locked up. It wasn't those rooms Cam was interested in anyway. It was the dark closet at the end of the hall. Something was pulling her there. And the door to that was wide open.

Cam stopped. Once more she mashed her back against the wall, trying to make herself invisible. It occurred to her, as her spine hit a quartet of insulated pipes running behind her, that someday, probably after their initiation, she and Alex might actually be able to do that. Cast some crystals, a pinch of herbs, mumble the right incantation, and *poof!*, they could hide in plain sight.

For now, however, they were uninitiated fledglings and, despite the fact that people were always saying how advanced they were, Cam didn't exactly feel like an expert at anything. Except maybe pushing past fear. If practice made perfect, she'd have that bad boy down in nothing flat.

The open door at the end of the hall hadn't budged. No light went on inside. No Witch Hunter came out. The coast was as clear as it was going to get. Cam dashed toward the closet.

She was barely in the door when she was hit by a spell of intense wooziness. She fell to her knees and, putting her hands out, she pitched forward. A canvas bag stopped her fall.

But not her dizziness.

The airless closet seemed to spin.

The ache started in her head. A tightening band of pain wound itself around her brow.

A vision. Just what she needed, she thought irritably. As if she weren't rattled enough, she was going to see something new, something bad. . . . Something, she realized, cringing with terror, that was pushing its way up through the leather-trimmed bag. . . .

His young wife and infant daughter had died in the crash. The crash that he had seen coming and done nothing to prevent. He had been driving and thinking. The radio talk show was merely background noise, like the sleet outside. As monotonous as the thumping windshield wiper. They were on their way to Appleton for Thanksgiving dinner with his in-laws.

He had been thinking how lucky he was. How miraculous it felt to be a father. How a few short months ago, he'd been just a lucky guy married to a beautiful, sweet-tempered girl; an ordinary man, he'd always thought, except for the fact that he had stronger hunches and intuitions than his friends, and that the probability of his premonitions being right was better than theirs. He felt things they did not — and wouldn't want to, considering the headaches that came along with those feelings.

Those were the ordinary thoughts he had until he noticed an eighteen-wheeler half a mile away on the other side of the highway. Saw its lights only, through slanted gusts of snow.

A sharp sting behind his eyes made him wince, he remembered.

His gloved hands tightened on the steering wheel.

What if? He found himself wondering as the stab of pain spread out like a mask behind his eyes. What if that truck on the other side of the highway, separated from them by a length of snow-covered turf and a low railing, suddenly skidded on the plowed highway?

What if, he lazily wondered, the massive truck, carrying a double-decker rack of new cars, hit a slick spot and jackknifed across the meridian?

The pain forced his eyes shut. What opened them was the crash. His car hitting or being hit by a bright, shiny electric-blue station wagon that had flown loose from its second-story moorings.

Helen, his adored young wife, was dead. Lydia, barely three months old, was dead. But he had survived. For what? Why had he lived when everything precious to him had died? Of what use would he be to anyone or anything ever again?

Elfman gave him an answer. Elfman, the meddling warlock he met two years after the crash.

The Witch Hunter had gone to a seminar about ESP. He had emerged from a terrible mourning period feeling useless but edgy. He was back at work, but his job no longer interested him. He felt as if he was searching for something or someone to burn up his restless energy.

A friend of his had read about the seminar and gotten him a ticket. Because, the friend said, he couldn't hide at home forever . . . and ESP, wasn't that what all those hunches and premonitions were? Didn't he want to find out more about it? About why he always knew what was going to happen when no one else in their crowd did?

He had not told the friend about seeing the deadly crash before it happened. He had told no one about spotting the massive truck looming through spears of sleet when it was much too far away for him to have really seen it.

But he went to the seminar. And there he met Elfman, the aptly named warlock. Small, wrinkled, white-bearded, with twinkling — yes, twinkling — water-pale eyes.

"Sami Elfman," he introduced himself in the lobby

during a break. "ESP is a gift, is it not?" he said, sounding casual, just making conversation.

"Or a curse," the hunter had responded.

"I'm sorry for your loss," Elfman said softly. "It was indeed a terrible loss. One that can never be forgotten or repaired. But your heart, broken as it may be, is still strong and open. And there are so many in the world who need its protection and care."

His head swam. How did the old man know about his loss? Or his heart? How could a stranger guess how he longed for a task, a cause, a mission — something to lose himself in. Or something to help him find himself again.

The bell sounded, signaling that the break was over. With an oddly comforting touch of his hand, Elfman scurried back into the auditorium and was, in an instant, lost in the crowd.

That had been in late November.

In early spring, he had gone to another event: a paranormal convention. He found himself searching the crowd for Elfman. It wasn't just a hunch he had that the old man would be there, it was a desire, an unexplainable need to see him.

"I have something for you," was the way the old warlock announced his presence. He took the hunter's arm and led him through the crowded aisles. There were dozens of exhibitors in the convention hall. A tiny Chinese woman, Lady Fan, Elfman called her, was manning the Herbal Health and Healing booth. She swept back a curtain at the rear of the cubicle and he and Elfman entered.

They talked for some time. But all he recalled of the conversation was that it began and ended similarly with the words, "A child needs you."

The child was a baby girl. An infant witch, Elfman said, who had been put up for adoption by her family. Before the astonished hunter could echo "an infant witch?" Elfman hurried on. Why would parents do such a thing? Because the child, at fourteen months, had proved . . . well, Elfman hemmed and hawed . . . precocious.

Precocious?

She seemed bright beyond her age, able to . . . well . . . do things a normal fourteen-month-old would be incapable of doing . . . things that even, say, a baby witch would not dream of doing.

There it was again. Tossed in as if it were nothing. Witch.

Elfman was vague as to exactly what precocious things the baby was able to do. But her parents, he continued, had grown nervous and uneasy around the tyke, he supposed. They had worried that they would not be able to take care of such a . . . such an advanced child. They had asked Elfman if he could find a better home for her.

That was, the warlock explained, shortly before they died. In a fire. From which the child was rescued. Well, actually, had Elfman mentioned that the child was . . . precocious?

Proof: She had crawled out of the house moments before it had collapsed.

CHAPTER THIRTEEN
A FRIEND IS WAITING

She didn't want to open the bag. It was all she could do to tear her clammy hands off it. Cam's palms were all pins and needles, vibrating painfully. She stood up. Her head was reeling with the awful dream, the nightmare that seemed to have seeped through the canvas. All she wanted to do was scrub her hands. Wash them clean of the Witch Hunter's story, and get home as fast as she could.

But something held her there, staring at the satchel. What was it holding, what was it hiding, that had released the twisted tale?

She unzipped the bag with trembling fingers. And there they were: a black robe and, in two pieces, the blade and the handle — the scythe the maniac had gripped at the premiere.

The Witch Hunter's hooded cloak and menacing weapon had been hidden in her school, in Mr. Golem's closet!

Shaken, Cam raced out of the building. On the school steps, she paused to gulp night air into her depleted lungs and thought she heard Alex calling to her.

Oh, please, Cam, please. Get home soon.

Oh, please? That didn't sound like her sister, Cam thought, wiping her hands on her boot-leg jeans as she rushed along the dusk-dark streets. A block from home, she heard it again. *Hurry. Please.* This time she recognized the voice.

Dave was in the hallway, carrying a cup of coffee, when Cam raced through the door. "Whoa," he called, protecting his cup, clutching it with two hands. "You have a visitor. In the den."

Before he asked the question, Cam answered it. "I'm okay. I'm fine. When did Sukari show up?"

Dave blinked at her, then shook his head. "Naw," he said, "I'm not even gonna go there. Yes, it's Sukari. And she got here about five minutes ago. I told her you were out. She said she'd wait. Said you wouldn't be long. I assumed you two had spoken."

Cam didn't bother to deny it. In a manner of speaking, she thought, they had "spoken." She had been able to hear her distressed friend's call.

Things really were changing; her powers were on the rise. It was a good thing, too, she thought. After her eerie experience in the boiler room closet, she could use all the magic she could muster.

Sukari was on her way to the den door when Cam entered the room. The tawny girl had a piece of paper in her hand. She threw her arms around Cam and whimpered, totally un-Suke-like, "I don't know what's going on. Oh, Cam, I need help. I'm scared. I think I'm going off the deep end."

"It's that kind of night," Cam couldn't help noting. A wave of comfort, of almost hyper-confidence, had washed away her trembling fear the minute she'd set foot inside the house. Being safely home, in the familiar surroundings of the den, knowing Dave was near and Emily somewhere upstairs, probably, was just what she needed. She hugged Sukari, then held the girl at arm's length. "I never thought I'd hear you say, 'I don't know what's going on.' Not you, AP answer girl —"

Sukari managed a shaky smile. "Yeah, you wouldn't think so, would you? Did you get one of these?" she asked cautiously, showing Cam the paper. It was a copy of the e-mail from the Witch Hunter.

"Of course," Cam answered. "See?" She pointed out the long list of people it had been sent to at the top of the page. "Everyone got it. It's someone's idea of a joke."

"But it says the Witch Hunter, Cam. It's from that nutcase at the premiere."

"Not. You've been hanging with Amanda too long, girlfriend." Cam turned away so Suke wouldn't see how sick it made her to flat out lie. "Where is gullible-girl, anyway?"

"I . . . I tried to tell her . . . I tried to explain," Sukari said miserably. "But she doesn't get it —"

"There's something about you Amanda doesn't get?" Cam laughed.

"Lately. Yeah." Sukari crushed the e-mail and threw it into her backpack. "I don't know where to begin," she said.

But she managed. Nervously, in stops and starts, half-sentences, and trailing thoughts, Sukari explained. When school started this year, she'd felt fine. Regular. She was psyched about getting into Spenser's Advanced Placement. She'd heard he was tough but supposedly a terrific teacher. And he had been, Sukari admitted. Totally terrific. Until . . .

Here, Sukari put her head in her hands. Until, she continued, she'd begun to know the answers to his tests —

"Well, duh, of course you would," Cam interrupted. "It's science. It's your subject."

"No, that's not it," Sukari protested. "I knew the answers before I actually saw the tests. I don't mean I knew-knew. I just sort of had a feeling about what he'd be asking. And I was right. Crazy right. It was as if I'd seen the tests in advance. I think that's what Spenser thinks. But I didn't. He kept asking me how I knew. And I kept saying it was just a feeling, you know? But even I knew it was more than that, Cam. It was like I was getting like you —"

Cam stiffened. "Like me? What do you mean?" she demanded, surprised at how defensive she sounded. Almost angry. Only it wasn't anger. It was the jumble of emotions — fear topping the list — that came whenever she realized, understood, or "got" something she didn't want to know.

And she'd just gotten who the Witch Hunter meant when he had said, "All three of you."

Sukari backed off. Literally. She took two steps back, then spun away from Cam. "Nothing. I don't know. I mean," she said, slowing down, trying to figure it out as she went along, "like your mojo, you know? You know, how you can feel things before they happen sometimes? Like in soccer, it's as if you can read the other team's mind; you guess exactly what play they'll make. . . . It's like that, Cam. I just have this feeling, this sense, about what's coming next. And it's freaking me to the max. But what's worse is, it's freaking Mr. Spenser, too. Last week, he called me a witch! In class. In front of everybody."

Cam, Alex, and Sukari made three.

Only Suke wasn't a witch. That much Cam was sure of.

"That jerk called you a witch in class? Inappropriate, bordering on harassment much? I'd report —"

Sukari paled. "No — I'm probably making too much of it. I don't want to cause a big thing. . . .

Cam sighed. *You didn't cause it,* she wanted to scream. Her mind raced. Sukari had come to her—somehow the AP ace had sensed, known, that if anyone could understand, Cam would. And be able to help. And isn't that what her gifts, her powers, were supposed to be for?

Cam gave humor a shot. "Okay, then, play along with him. Bring a Nimbus 2000 to class tomorrow."

Swing and a miss. Sukari's eyes were beginning to fill with tears. Time to get real.

She didn't go into all of it. She talked about how some people — without mentioning Dave, or Alex's adoptive mom, Sara, or others she and Als had run into — were just hyper-aware, supersensitive to what was going on around them. Their radar was keener, their instincts sharper, their intuition dead-on.

"Like you," Suke said.

"Um, yeah, sort of," Cam responded. She'd half expected Sukari to argue or ask how she knew all this, or insist on proof. But the stressed-out girl was just grateful to hear that she was not alone.

Cam didn't discuss the hierarchy. Didn't say that these people were called Sensitives.

Or that they were capable of rearing and protecting fledgling witches and warlocks, but not of becoming one.

Or that, when a Sensitive accepted a fledgling to rear, he or she became a Protector.

Rearing and protecting? Cam shuddered violently. Without thinking, she rubbed her still-clammy hands together. And wisps of the Witch Hunter's story seemed to rise out of them.

He'd known the truck was going to crash. Like Dave, he'd met a witch, probably a tracker, at a healing and magic convention. And he had been given a fledgling witch to rear. So he had gone from Sensitive to Protector.

But what had happened? Why had he turned against all witches?

"I'm a scientist," Sukari was saying. "My dad's a doctor, my mom's a researcher. How am I supposed to accept this . . . this . . ."

"This gift," Cam finally said. She sat down on the

den's beat-up leather sofa and pulled Sukari onto the cushion next to her. "Okay, listen up," she said, hanging on to the stressed girl's cold hands. She explained gently, lightly, leaving lots out, what a blessing it could be to kinda "know" things, sense stuff. . . . Especially, Cam added, if you were a scientist. She reminded Suke of the banner posted in their ninth grade science class: IMAGINATION IS MORE IMPORTANT THAN KNOWLEDGE. A quote from Albert Einstein.

Sukari was nodding, buying it, squeezing Cam's hands gratefully. "I've always been very intuitive," she agreed. "And empathetic. My dad says that's what will make me a great doctor." Then, all of a sudden, she shook her head and leaped up. "Okay. Let's say I accept your premise. That this sudden mojo gift is a good thing. Then why is it bugging Mr. Spenser so much?"

What had Karsh told them once? When you point a finger, you've got three pointing back at you. And Ileana? She'd said something similar: If you can name it, you can claim it.

Spenser had seen something of himself in Sukari, something he obviously didn't like.

The same must be true of the Witch Hunter, Cam realized. He must have experienced something upsetting, too. Something to do with witches. With the infant witch the tracker Elfman had placed in his care . . .

And then she knew. It was so obvious. So easy. The scent of chem lab they kept smelling. How could she not have guessed? Alex was right. Mr. Golem wasn't the Witch Hunter. . . .

Cam could hardly wait to dash upstairs and tell her sister what had happened in the school basement, and what she'd finally figured out.

But as she walked Sukari to the door, the girl said, "One more thing. Cam, how come it's happening now? Why did I suddenly start getting all these . . . feelings, the premonitions and stuff, this semester? It doesn't make sense, does it?"

Not unless, Cam thought, you were a twin who'd been scared and lonely but hiding behind this mask of raging popularity — until your other half showed up to make you whole . . . and to jack up the powers you'd always had but were too afraid to use for anything but helping a pal or winning a soccer game.

Proximity. That was the answer. Nearness. Being with another who shared your gift could set in motion a whole new level of skill.

That's what had happened for her and Alex.

It was happening to Sukari because of Mr. Spenser.

CHAPTER FOURTEEN
THE SCENT OF EVIL

"Alex!" Cam burst into their room.

"Yo, take it down a thousand. I can hear you," Dylan shouted from under Cam's headphones. "When did you get here? Where'd you go?"

"Never mind that. Take off those headphones. They're mine. And where's Alex?"

"Whew. Not too stingy, are you?" Dylan said sourly, slipping off the phones. "She's out looking for you."

"When did she leave?" Cam asked, alarmed.

Her brother fingered the headphones casually and craned his neck, looking up, as if he were concentrating deeply, trying to find the answer on the ceiling. "Hmmm, when? When?"

"Okay, take the headphones. You've got 'em. Take them to your room. Listen to rap until your ears blow off, okay? Now when did Alex leave?"

Dylan scrambled happily to his feet. "Ten, fifteen minutes ago," he said. "Can I borrow a couple of CDs?"

"Why? Got more news for me?" Cam grumbled.

"About two vintage Pearl Jams' worth," Dylan confessed. "Jason was here, too. He left with Alex."

She had to lose him.

It was their third time around Half Moon Cove. Jason's headlights swept the fog-shrouded beach looking for her sister.

"My bad," Alex said again. "It was just a guess, Jase. Obviously a wrong one. Cam's not here. She's probably at home by now."

Getting rid of Jason was proving stickier than bubble gum on a shoe sole. Alex's mistake had been to tell him, one, that she was on her way out; and two — just to get him out of the way — that Cam might be at Half Moon Cove. And what had the lanky dude done? Offered her a lift if she drove out with him.

Okay. So she had. And now she had to shake him and get on with the night's nefarious activities. She had to get him safely away from her. She needed to find Cam. And the obvious place to look — without the Earl of B-ball at her side — was Golem's subterranean sanctuary. Cam was so convinced it was him.

"Guess you're right." Jason gave in at last. He whirled the steering wheel and pointed his car up one of the winding cobblestone streets that led away from the water. "Okay, we'll head back."

"You," Alex corrected him. "I've got to stop at the school —"

"Now? Time check, Alex. The place will be locked up tight."

"Telling time never was my strong point." Alex crossed her arms and sat in the front seat, steaming at her own stupidity.

They were headed away from the cove, driving slowly through narrow lanes thick with summer fog, when something thudded against the front of the car. "What the —?" Jason murmured.

I second that emotion, Alex thought. *What the?* is right.

Jason had lurched forward. He was shaken, but okay.

Alex opened her door and jumped out to investigate. Lit by the headlights, something fuzzy and black, a big bag or rag or blanket, was heaped on the ground in front of the car. It reminded her of the Witch Hunter's costume.

She knelt to see it better, to touch it.

It was velvet. Dark, but not black.

The cloth was purple. It wasn't the sweet, soft purple of violets, Sara's favorite flower, but a deeper shade like the sleep-inducing valerian in Ileana's herb garden, or the vivid-colored berries on deadly nightshade.

Purple. The color of Sersee's eyes, Alex remembered.

With foreboding, she lifted the cloth — and knew before it was completely unfurled that it was a cape.

Velvet. Violet. Like Sersee's cape.

The feel of cold fingers dancing down her spine paralyzed Alex for a moment. Then she heard a tinkling noise, like icy laughter.

She spun around. But the evil young witch was not there. Only fog and pealing echoes filled the dark road.

No one was laughing, Alex tried to tell herself. More likely she had heard wind chimes. Lots of the "quaint" houses near the waterfront sported wind chimes and cherubs in their gardens.

Shuddering, Alex balled up the cape and flung it away into the darkness. Caught by a sudden breeze, the sleek fabric twisted and skittered across the road like a feral creature. It rolled through bushes, rattling trash cans in its path.

"What was that? What did we hit?" Jason wanted to know when Alex got back into the car.

"Nothing. A . . . a garbage can lid. It . . . it must've rolled into the road. Jase, go home, now. Drop me at Allen Street and please, please, go home."

"But what about Cam?" he asked.

It was startling how good she was getting at lying. "I just talked to her," she blithely replied; never mind that she didn't have a cell phone or beeper with her. "She's at your place. I mean, she's on her way. She'll meet you over there."

"You're sure you'll be okay?" Jase asked a few minutes later, as Alex scooted out of his car.

Another smooth lie. "Totally," she said.

She was prepared to throw a rock through one of the high windows of the gym, or to smash the front door glass. It wasn't necessary. The back door, the one leading into the sports center, was wide open.

And there were cars in the staff lot. Nearly a dozen of them.

Was there a teachers' conference going on?

Whatever, Alex thought. Her good luck. She and Cam were due for some.

She slipped into the gym, then dashed out into the corridor, mindlessly following the trace scent of Cam's ginger-tea shampoo. As she'd guessed, it led her toward the fire door to the basement, to Golem World.

Should she hurry down the stairs to find Cam, or check out the classroom that her delicate new tracking instinct told her might be the Witch Hunter's true lair?

As if to settle the dilemma, another smell, familiar and frightening, singed her nostrils. A repulsive and grating brew of odors: iodine, garlic, sulfuric acid, rubbing alcohol — all swirling in a burnt milk stench.

Alex turned away from the basement door and followed her nose. And her intuition. They led her, as she had thought they might, down the deserted corridor, past the senior lockers, to the door of Mr. Spenser's classroom.

CHAPTER FIFTEEN
A COVEN OF HUNTERS

Through the frosted-glass pane, Alex could make out dark shapes: a group of people milling near the blackboard. She pushed the door gently. And might as well have kicked it in. The un-lubed hinges squealed. Everyone in the room turned toward the sound. The door was abruptly yanked open. And Alex faced the Witch Hunter.

Times ten.

Pandemonium broke out as an army of black-robed figures caught sight of her. Some pulled up their hoods, panicked. Others stared at her with terrifying malice.

At the blackboard, Mr. Spenser shook off his hood and glared at Alex. "I would say, what a surprise," he crooned, "except that nothing you and your kind do surprises me anymore. Come in, Ms. Fielding." He beckoned her with a hand still clasping chalk.

On the blackboard behind him, Alex saw her name. Hers and Cam's and . . . Sukari's. Each was enclosed in a chalked circle. Lines, like balloon strings, led from their names to a single oversized word: witches!

"Sukari? Wake up and smell the mocha java," Alex blurted. "I know Sukari Woodward. And she's no witch."

"Grab her," Spenser ordered.

Two of the mob seized her arms and dragged her toward him. A third costumed creep prodded her forward. Spenser snapped on a pair of sterile gloves before he touched her. His large, skinny hand was cold on the back of her neck. His fingers reached around to clamp her jugular.

"This is what we're about," he announced. "This innocent-looking child —"

Alex had never heard herself described that way. She felt like giggling. Except that his claws were pinching her neck. And that was no laughing matter. She shook her head but he only squeezed harder. Which angered more than scared her.

"This mere fourteen-year-old —"

"Fifteen," Alex shot back. "Sixteen in October. Halloween, actually. You guys want to come to my party? I mean, you're dressed for it."

One of the men who had Alex's arm shook her. "Witchling, be silent!"

"Witchling?" Alex couldn't help it. "Where are you guys from, the SciFi channel?"

"Silence," Spenser railed predictably. "The bewitched girls of Salem were mere children, too. As was my own adopted daughter!"

His daughter? This was news. She hadn't thought about Spenser having kids. Why would she? She hadn't thought of him at all until Sukari started getting all flustered around him.

No wonder Suke had flipped out. The weirdo thought she was a witch.

Alex tried to turn to look over her shoulder at Mr. Spenser, but he kept her facing out, displaying her to his pals like a freak-show exhibit. She'd wanted to check his expression, to see whether he'd heard her think of him as a weirdo.

Interesting, she thought now. He can't read minds. He has no real power. Just that dumb robe and funky hood to hide behind.

There was still no reaction from him. Which comforted her. Still, she wished he'd let go of her neck. "Can I ask you something?" she said, as if they were in class together and she didn't understand a formula he'd just drawn on the board. "What's your issue with witches? I mean, how come you hate them so much? Why are you coming after us *now*?"

There was a hue and cry in the room. "Witches are the devil's spawn!" someone shouted. "They recruit the innocent!" This from another Halloweenie. "They eat children!"

"Well, the school cafeteria does serve some obscure meats, but I wouldn't go that far." Alex tried not to laugh.

"This is not a joke," Spenser announced. Alex finally wriggled around to look at him. His eyes narrowed. He was staring at her as if she were a frog waiting to be dissected. Which did not comfort her.

While his cohorts shouted out their grievances against witches and warlocks, Alex tried to make sense of what she'd heard. Okay. Mr. Spenser had a daughter. The adopted girl was — or had been — a witch? Like us, Alex thought, like Cam and me. But weren't fledglings supposed to be adopted by Sensitives?

So that was it, she concluded. Mr. Spenser was a Sensitive. That's how he'd picked up their vibes in the first place. He didn't actually know they were witches. He was guessing.

And what about this daughter of his? Had he harmed her? Killed her? Did the man hate witches so much that he'd destroyed the one he was supposed to take care of?

Sorry, Artemis, a recognizable voice said. *It was I who destroyed him.*

Alex shuddered. "Sersee?" she asked cautiously.

A chill went through the room. It was as if something cold and invisible had circled the lab in a rush. Capes flared. Hair fluttered. Alex felt her bare arms erupt in goose bumps. But no one and nothing was visible. Not to her. And definitely not to the coven of witch hunters. Looking stupefied, stumped, they were watching Spenser.

He whirled Alex around and stared intently at her. "How do you know that name?" he demanded.

Where was that quick creative tongue when she needed it, Alex thought desperately. Okay, the guy couldn't read her mind. Couldn't frizzle her hair with his eyeballs. Probably didn't know a charm from an incantation. But that didn't mean that he and his after-school mates weren't dangerously deranged.

"Sersee. You said 'Sersee,' didn't you?" the science teacher shouted.

"She did. I heard her." One of the bug-eyed witch busters pointed at Alex.

Sersee, the despicable little demon who'd held them captive on Coventry, was Mr. Spenser's daughter? Alex was floored.

"Answer, witch!" he railed at her.

"Answer or die!" One of the men in the crowd,

short, round, bald, with a wispy mustache, threw back his cloak and drew a hunting knife from a tooled leather holder on his belt.

The holster had probably netted Tweedle-dee an A in shop. "Are you serious?" Alex blurted at the belligerent boob.

"If he's not, I am," another knife-wielding, robed fiend offered.

No. Don't. The order came directly from the boss. Only Spenser hadn't bothered to say it aloud. He'd thought it. And after that, Alex picked up on another thought of his. *This is going too far.*

Our job is to expose, not to execute. Don't they understand, we must not become like them.

Yo, Harpo! Alex sent a desperate message to the science teacher. *Say it aloud, okay?*

No dice. Spenser hadn't heard her thought memo. He couldn't. He wasn't a witch. But Sersee was. And she, apparently, had intercepted Alex's anxious request. And was now cackling with cruel delight.

"How do you know my daughter?!" Spenser was shaking her again.

"Ask her yourself," Alex shouted back. "She's here."

Spenser was losing it — if someone who was already certifiably crazy had anything left to lose, Alex thought. Fact was, his precious daughter *was* there.

Somewhere. She was making her taunting presence felt every way but visibly.

There was that nasty cackle and the cape Alex had found in front of Jason's car. The scary rush of wind through the lab. And most of all, Alex knew she had not hallucinated it. She had heard the despicable girl speak a minute ago. *It was I who destroyed* him, Sersee had bragged.

"Answer me, witch! How do you know my lost daughter?!" Spenser shook her so hard she could feel her brain rattling in its pan. But jolted as she was, Alex's eyes could still focus on the metallic glint of knives pointed at her.

Where was her weapon-melting sister when she needed her?

The question brought another malicious cackle from the out-of-sight skank.

Skank? Sersee silently roared.

Skank, scuzz, loser, miserable misfit, rebellious little reject, daughter of a wack-job witch hunter, Alex thought deliberately, trying to smoke the violet-eyed troublemaker out into the open.

One of the jars on Spenser's shelves exploded. It was the one that had held some nameless organism that looked like a giant, peeled garlic bobbing in phlegm. Out of that noxious ooze, appropriately enough it seemed to

Alex, Sersee appeared — a monstrous lab experiment gone wrong.

"Kill her!" the furious witch ordered. "Call yourselves witch hunters? Ha!"

Spenser leaped between his crew and Alex. "No!" he shouted at last. "That is not our purpose or our right."

"Right, shmight," Sersee taunted him. "That was always your thing. What's right and wrong. What's good and bad. Well, you found out, didn't you? Me, that's what was wrong and bad. And you, poor papa of mine, you were always right and good."

The cloaked witch hunters had backed away from Spenser and Alex and were cringing before Sersee, who was violently pacing, her robes flaring, her thick black hair swirling with each abrupt move.

"Illusion. It was all illusion," Sersee screeched, turning on Spenser. "You were not good and certainly not right. You actually believed that I had murdered my parents. You never said it aloud. You never admitted it to me. Gutless dolt, I could read your thoughts when I was two! And before that I saw the way you looked at me. As though I were a dangerous animal and not an abandoned, orphaned child."

Spenser's hands were shaking violently. From where she stood, Alex could see the color rise in his neck . . . and drain from his face as he turned suddenly to look at her. His mouth moved as if to speak, but nothing came out. It frightened Alex badly, more than the knives, more than Sersee.

She wondered if his wayward daughter had cast a spell on him. Or whether Mr. Spenser might be having a stroke. He looked very ill.

The other witch hunters noticed it, too. They began to point and mumble and chatter like treed chimpanzees.

"You were supposed to protect me," Sersee shrilled at her father. "But you feared me instead. And that fear, your panic and dread, taught me more about myself than all the false words of praise you offered."

Mr. Spenser lost his footing, but found his voice. He sank to his knees before Sersee. "Is that why you left me?" he asked shakily.

"What better reason?" the young witch demanded coldly.

"If you could read my mind," Spenser said very softly, "could you not see, know, understand that, despite my fears, I loved you? Can you ever forgive me?"

"In a word of one syllable," the enraged witch declared, "no. But I can't waste my time with you. Leave here. Now. This minute." She stamped her foot. "And never again toy with witches or warlocks. Never look upon their faces. Never dare call us by name!"

Spenser stood slowly. His back was hunched with

sorrow, his head down. As he walked out the classroom door, his supporters shouted to him, cursed him, cried out that he was deserting them.

Sersee spun suddenly, her hands extended like claws. "Shut up," she commanded the jabbering witch hunters, "before I turn you all into rodents! You wouldn't last long in a laboratory, would you?"

They shrank back as one.

"Weaklings. Bullies. You hide inside your robes while I exalt in mine. What should I do with you?" she demanded of the trembling rabble. "Rats are too daring, snakes too clever, cats too independent . . . while you are meek, stupid followers. Individually, you are nothing; only in a mob do you dare to act."

One of Spenser's men keeled over in fear. A second reached to help him but checked Sersee's face for permission and thought better of it. "Tell us," another begged, "what we can do for you? It's not witches we hate. It's just . . . certain kinds of . . . witches."

"Oh?" Sersee paraded before the terrified man. "What kind is that?"

"Only the evil ones," another man called out in a quavering voice.

"Evil ones? Idiots! What do you know of evil?!" Her eyes scanned the room as if she was seeking an example. They landed on Alex and narrowed, judging, appraising.

Alex shrank back against the blackboard, desperately trying to scramble her thoughts, her fear, from the menacing witch.

"I've got it," Sersee declared. Glee lit her large violet eyes. "You want to taunt 'a certain kind' of witch or warlock? An evil one?" she challenged the petrified pack. "Well, I know just the brute —"

CHAPTER SIXTEEN
SERSEE'S REVENGE

The witch hunters swept out of the classroom, hurrying to catch up with Sersee, who was howling with laughter.

A moment later, Cam rushed in, pale as paper. "You're okay?! Oh my god, Als. You have no idea what I thought — what I just saw — what I thought I saw!"

"Nothing wrong with your eyes, Chamomile." Alex allowed her sister to hug her feverishly, then allowed herself to hug Cam back. "She was here. Sersee. Spenser is, or used to be, her Protector."

Floored, Cam gasped, "Mr. Spenser and Sersee?! Get out."

"He was also the Witch Hunter," Alex said.

"I figured that out. Sukari came by. Als, he thinks she's a witch." Cam stopped abruptly and stepped back. "Did you say 'was'?" Belatedly she'd picked up on the fine distinction.

"Spenser. Yes. He *was* the Witch Hunter. Totally past tense. Sersee fired him. It was pitiful —"

"Not half as pitiful as that mob of morons running after her," Cam noted. "Where's she taking them? What were they doing here? Was Spenser throwing a Mr. Witch Hunter contest at Marble Bay High?"

"She's going to sic them on some poor slob who she says is really evil." Alex shook her head. "Can you imagine how bad someone has to be for Sersee to think they're evil? Um, excuse me?" It was Alex's turn to be slow on the uptake. "Did you say you figured out that Zany Brainy was the Witch Hunter?"

"Spenser, yeah." Cam nodded. "Let's get out of here."

"Yo, Lucy," Alex teased, throwing an arm over her sister's shoulder and heading for the door, "I think you've got some s'plainin' to do —"

Ileana was impressed. Not by the shining steel-and-glass architecture of Massachusetts CompUMag, or by the carefully clipped trees and shrubs in front of it, or the spotless circular drive leading up to the building, but by the fact that she and Miranda, working together, had achieved liftoff.

They'd used a basic locator spell to find Thantos. That part was easy. Elementary. Then they'd stood on Coventry's shore like a pair of beginners, peering across the water at the mainland and wondering when the next ferry would arrive. Finally, Miranda, reading the younger witch's thoughts, had glanced at Ileana and said, "Well, shall we?"

Okay, so it had taken three tries. But they'd finally gotten the traveling spell right. Right herbs. Right crystals. Right incantation. And, most important, right thinking. When they had rid themselves of anger, selfish motives, and desire for revenge, the charm worked like a charm.

The proof? Here they were, witches on a mission, standing before the tidy glass doors of the hulking trickster's headquarters.

"Getting here was the easy part," Miranda reminded Ileana. "Now we have to find Karsh's journal. That is, if that horrible little witch wasn't lying about giving it to Thantos."

"She was too ticked off to lie," was Ileana's opinion. "Imagine, she gave him the book hoping he'd take her under his wing, prop up her power, teach her tracker secrets. And the sly skunk accepted the gift and said thank you by disabling her. He's got the journal. I'm certain of it."

"I was just thinking," Miranda began.

Ileana cut her off curtly. "Hello, I know what you were just thinking and there's no time now."

"But we're so near —"

"First the book, then your babies, okay? There'll be time enough to visit Cam and Alex later. For goodness' sake, Miranda, stay focused."

They entered the spacious lobby, their sandaled feet clicking over the flawless marble floor. A burly man in a spick-and-span dark blue suit, a security tag dangling from a gleaming chain and an earpiece trailing wire down his neck, stopped them and asked to see their ID.

"I'm Mr. DuBaer's sister-in-law," Miranda offered, smiling politely.

"And I'm his daughter," Ileana groused.

"And I'm his mother's third cousin once removed," the immaculate rent-a-cop sneered. "No ID, no entry. Get it, girls?"

"Once removed? I'll show you once removed," Ileana snapped, fishing for the piece of iron pyrite in the leather pouch at her belt. Pyrite for deception, for making things disappear. She'd have settled for the tektite, which sucked up bad energy like a Hoover.

"Oh, please, allow me." Miranda's cool hand landed gently on Ileana's wrist. Smiling all the while, the older witch stared directly into the big man's little eyes. Which, at once, began to water. Then from the pocket of her long robe, she withdrew a handful of herbs. She opened her palm under the blinking guard's bulbous nose and allowed him to stare stupidly at the green flakes.

"Together?" Miranda asked Ileana without turning her head.

"Make a wish." Ileana laughed. And together they blew the herbs into the man's face. "Ta-ta." Miranda fluttered her now-empty fingers at him.

"Sleep tight," Ileana crooned, slipping the pyrite into his handkerchief pocket a moment before he fell over backward, making the polished floor quake.

Thantos felt the tremor two stories up.

He'd been sitting at his gleaming mahogany desk, flipping through Karsh's worthless story — his futile attempt to unseat Thantos and turn the dynasty over to the DuBaer women.

With growing anger, he had been rereading the part about how he, as a boy, had urged his father to investigate the caves of Coventry. The caves in which his father had been ambushed and killed. Slain, old Karsh insisted, by one of the traitorous, deranged, and derelict warlocks who lurked underground.

It was a pity that no one but Karsh and the murderer had witnessed the act. The mad culprit was long dead. Thantos had seen to that years ago. And now the ancient tracker was dead, too. Delicious irony. Thantos's own nephews, his imbecile brother Fredo's sons, had taken care of that.

Only they, two dead men, had heard Nathaniel's last words. The words that had ripped the DuBaer dynasty from its rightful heirs, Nathaniel's sons — Aron, Fredo, and the only one left with the brains and brawn to claim it, Thantos.

According to Karsh, Nathaniel had placed his family and its fortune in the care of his granddaughters. Only females would head the family. Females immune to the Antayus Curse.

Which left out Thantos's own ungrateful child, Ileana, since her long-dead mother had been an Antayus. But left in his brother Aron's troublesome twins, Camryn and Alexandra. Miranda's children. Wild girls who had not even been reared on Coventry and had not yet been initiated.

They never would be, Thantos vowed. Not while he lived.

He had just taken a deep, calming breath. He had

just tapped the passage with his forefinger — the passage that spoke of who had killed his father underground. There it was. His way out. Then the hair on the nape of his neck bristled, signaling that enemies were near.

Thantos sniffed once, lavishly, as if he were testing the quality of tobacco in a fine cigar. Crisp air, mingled with juniper berries and evergreen needles, came first to his nostrils. It was the unmistakable scent of Coventry.

Sersee, he thought. He had left the girl on the sea cliff, her pale betrayed face pointing toward the battering wind. He looked around his spacious office for a place to hide the book.

It was too late. As he scanned the pleasingly uncluttered space, the locked doors before him flew back. Instead of the vengeful urchin, he faced two agitated women. One was the gentle, beautiful, and gullible mother of the twins, his rivals; the other, their guardian, his own hotheaded offspring, Ileana.

A broad and surprisingly earnest smile erased his startled look.

These two he could deal with. Always had. Although he was less than pleased that Miranda, who had always been so open, admiring, and accepting of him, had taken up with his bone-hard brat. It was more than a nuisance, actually. It was almost a threat.

As was his custom, Thantos tuned into Miranda's mind. What he heard — or didn't hear — emptied his smile of sincerity. She had closed the door against him. Miranda, who had trusted him unwaveringly since Aron's death, was scrambling her thoughts. Shutting him out.

"Yes, well, it's always nice to have a visit from family," he said, struggling to disguise his displeasure. "You must be tired. It's a long way from Coventry."

"We took a shortcut," his snotty daughter snapped.

Miranda, he noticed, took the girl's hand. "Thantos," she said in the light, whispery voice he adored, "I've just seen something terrible. And been told something worse. Of course, I can't believe it of you —"

Ileana snorted sarcastically but held her tongue.

"I can't imagine what you mean. Sit. Please." Thantos set down the book as casually as if it were a computer magazine he'd been browsing. He put it on his tidy desk and pretended to shuffle through a few papers, which he then placed over Karsh's journal. He had not so much disguised the pages as hidden them in plain sight, then he turned back to face his guests.

"We found a girl, a child —" Miranda began.

"Sersee," Ileana cut in.

"Sersee?" Thantos's expression didn't change but his dark eyes glinted angrily. "I don't believe I know anyone by that name."

"Oh, yeah, well she knows you, Big Daddy."

The hand holding Ileana's administered a knuckle-busting squeeze. "She told us a very distressing story," Miranda continued.

Thantos stroked his beard. "Sersee, Sersee," he tested the name. "I think I recall the girl now. A homeless waif, a liar, and a thief. She and her friends, the Furies, they call themselves, have been pillaging the island for years."

"A liar and a thief? Well, you'd know, wouldn't you? If you can name it, you can claim it," Ileana hissed.

Like an incensed bull, Thantos's thick shoulders reared up. His arm swung back. Miranda jumped in front of Ileana to block the blow. But the exasperated tracker turned away from both of them and brought his fist crashing down on his desk.

The papers he'd spread over Karsh's book flew up. The cover flipped open. Inside its hollow shell sat the precious pages.

"That's mine!" Ileana roared, rushing forward.

"Then take it!" Thantos tore the pages from their nest and flung them at his daughter.

Miranda gasped. Thantos turned on her with a look of such rage that she put up her hands involuntarily, as if to protect herself from him.

He saw her wince and recoil. He turned away again, trying to calm down and to think — which for Thantos meant only one thing — to work out a way to regain his advantage.

It infuriated him that Miranda had witnessed his loss of control. He blamed it on Ileana. And on his daughter's mewling guardian, Karsh Antayus.

The Antayus Curse had destroyed dozens of DuBaer men. That was why Nathaniel, Thantos's own father, had decided that only women should head the dynasty. Well, here, Thantos thought, striking his own thick chest, was one man the curse would fail to crush. But he needed Miranda on his side.

"Forgive me," he said, the moment he saw that it was his only option.

Dramatically, he grasped her hands. "Miranda, please forgive my outburst, my terrible temper, my frustration. You must know I would never harm you or your children. It was for you and for them that I wanted to read Karsh's words. I was going to give his journal to you as soon as I had finished it. I took it to make certain it did not fall into the hands of one who would use it badly. Misuse it to cause a rift between us. To sow doubt and fear in you. To turn you against me."

He paused to glare at Ileana, but she barely noticed

him now. She was wiping the soiled book with the hem of her skirt. At the sight of Karsh's familiar cramped writing, her eyes had filled with tears.

Thantos threw her a contemptuous look, then turned back to Miranda. "I took the book from my own daughter only to help you. I took it from Ileana. Yes. From an Antayus whose hatred of DuBaers is in her blood —"

An audacious hoot interrupted him. He turned toward the sound, toward the doors Ileana and Miranda had flung open. In the wide frame stood Sersee, laughing and pointing at him.

"Who took the book?" she howled. "Not you, coward. Not you, too noble to sully your hands. It was I, the lowly orphan you thought you could destroy!"

She flew past him, her cape sailing out behind her, and rapped on the pane of the enormous window behind his desk.

A commotion started up from below. A strange chanting that only Sersee seemed to understand. The trio, Thantos, Miranda, and Ileana, rushed to join her at the window.

Two stories below, they saw a riot in progress. A horde of strangers in black capes and hoods trudged before the building, waving sticks, fists, and primitive-looking swords. Some were in hand-to-hand combat with Thantos's security force. Others were tearing up the carefully pruned trees and bushes in front of the building. Still others were collaring terrified workers who had run out to see what was happening.

Thantos saw some of his employees look up, following the accusing fingers of the bizarrely robed rabble. They, too, his own workers, began to shake their fists and shout at him. But their voices were muffled by the thick glass.

Sersee realized the problem in an instant. Turning, she grabbed a large metal disk that had been sitting on Thantos's desk. A bear wearing a crown was etched into the heavy paperweight. She recognized it as the DuBaer crest.

Thantos made a move to take it from her. But it was too late. The lightning-quick imp hurled the disk at the window. The huge pane shattered. The impact sent fat splinters of glass across his tidy desk, ripping ugly scars in the polished mahogany, tattering and scattering his neat piles of paper like so much confetti across the once pristine room.

Thantos lunged at the brazen urchin. But stopped suddenly. Burning with rage, he heard the insolent, incredibly embarrassing cry from below:

"Thantos DuBaer is a witch! He lives a lie! Warlock, your time has come!"

CHAPTER SEVENTEEN
HELLO, GOOD-BYE

No place was safe. It was as simple as that.

Not Coventry, the island of their birth and bloodlines. Not Marble Bay, the picture-postcard, "nothing bad ever happens here" town where Cam had grown up and Alex found sanctuary.

Anyplace people feared and hated what they didn't understand — including ordinary people with heightened senses or a talent for making the scientifically impossible possible — was no longer a DMZ, a zone of safe space. And that was pretty much everywhere, Cam found herself thinking.

It was the last day of school. Students poured out of Marble Bay High, cheering and laughing, flushed with summer freedom. As Cam's footsteps echoed through the almost empty halls, she fought the urge to look over her shoulder, to listen for anyone following her, to give in to the creeping paranoia that could, if she let it, become a way of life.

Much as she tried to stifle it, one notion hung on. She wasn't alone. Her suspicion blossomed as she noticed that the door to the chem lab was open.

A moment before she reached it, she realized who she'd find there.

Sukari.

With relief, Cam saw her friend slumped in her front row seat, staring at her report card.

"You didn't fail, did you?" she asked softly, so as not to startle the engrossed girl.

"A-plus in science," Sukari confirmed in a monotone. She did not look up.

"You miss him?" Cam posed it as a question, but it wasn't a question. Shuddering, she knew. In her hazy way she could still read Suke's mind. And it was all about the Witch Hunter and loss.

"Who, Mr. Spenser?" Sukari shrugged.

"Suke, he was . . . kind of . . . creepy, wasn't he? Out-there and abusive. He called you a witch —"

Suke hoisted her plump self out of the chair. "Well, I'm not a witch anymore," she said, sighing.

"You never were," Cam reminded her.

"Maybe not." Sukari stood and shouldered her back-pack. "But even though it was freaky, there was something kind of cool about guessing his questions in advance. I don't know why he started flipping out. I heard he's in, like, some hospital or rest home or something. But talk about chemistry — we had it, Mr. Spenser and I." She smiled sadly. "Something tells me my mojo days are gone. With the dude who took his place . . . it's back to our regularly scheduled knowing-by-studying program."

Jason stuck his head in the door. "There you are," he said to Cam. "Thought we had a date."

"We do." Cam patted Sukari's back. "Come with?" she asked.

"Rain check," Suke demurred. "Hey, Jase. When are you leaving?"

"Tomorrow." He opened his arms to her. "Come on, give me a good-bye hug."

Suke reached up and hugged him. "Everyone's going . . . or gone," she said.

With no advance warning, not a mojo tickle, Cam burst into tears.

Alex charged by the open door, then backed up to look inside. "Yo, last day of school. It's no-cry Friday. Didn't you get the memo?"

"Guess some of us don't see the 'good' in good-bye," Cam offered, laughing despite herself.

"Run that by me again," her sister proposed.

"Well, Jason's leaving —"

"And Cade's coming tomorrow. Yahoo!" Alex shouted.

Would she recognize him? Would he know her? The last time she'd seen him her hair had been . . . platinum? Red-tipped? Streaked blue? She couldn't recall.

Cade's flight from London was scheduled to land at the opposite end of the terminal from the jet that would be winging Jason west.

Alex figured she'd catch him at the international passengers' passport check. She was anxious to get over there, eager to split from Cam, who was working overtime trying to keep it light and breezy. But it was Cam's barely holdin' it together 'tude that kept Alex glued to her sister's side.

Pacing outside security, waiting for Jase and his 'rents to arrive, Cam was reciting a mumbled monologue of reassurances. "It's no real biggie, is it?" "He'll be back in a couple of months, right?" "There's always e-mail —"

The mumblings were supposedly addressed to Alex but were actually a one-way pep talk Cam was giving herself.

Which made Alex's presence kind of unnecessary. You would think. Only Cam wouldn't let her leave. She kept insisting that she needed Alex's input.

Alex slumped down in her molded plastic seat. It was attached by a metal bar to her twin's identical tangerine chair. Of course nothing was in or on Cam's seat at the moment but her silvery, see-through backpack. The bar bolting the chairs together? Pointless, Alex thought, since she and Cam were linked by more than steel.

"I mean, I love the guy, but it's not like I'm *in* love with him —"

Alex failed to see the distinction and tried, for the umpteenth time, to make her presence — and her desire to split — evident to her diving-off-the-deep-end sib.

Why had she let Cam talk her into borrowing a pair of fresh stonewashed jeans and a sparkly belly-baring tee instead of slipping into the time-worn black denims and aged leather jacket that fit and felt like a second skin?

Would Cade have changed his look, she wondered. Would he be duded up in some trendy Eurotrash outfit? Maybe he had mowed his long black hair with its floppy strands falling over his forehead?

"Are you okay?" she asked Cam, for the third — fourth? fifth? — time that morning.

"Hello." Cam put her hands on her hips and cocked her head at Alex. "Why do you keep asking that?"

"Oh, hey, look. There he is. Here they come." Alex leaped up at the sight of Jason heading toward them. "Catchya later." She went to buzz Cam on the cheek for luck.

Way wrong move.

Cam grabbed her hand and clamped it tight. "Don't go. Wait with me. I need your moral support."

"And I need my digits!" Alex nearly shouted, yanking back her hand. "You're fine — like you've been telling me all day. You're okay. You'll be okay. To quote a gross commercial, 'gotta go, gotta go, gotta go right now.'"

Alex bolted over to Jason, threw her arms around the towering hottie, and said her own good-bye. Then she wheeled away from the emotional train wreck that used to be her tranquil twin and took off for the international terminal. . . .

Where her own much-delayed meltdown commenced.

According to the blinking light on the departures and arrivals monitor, the London flight had landed. Cade Richman was home.

Alex began to pace furiously outside the immigration and passport area. How long would it take for people to gather their belongings and leave the plane? Not that long . . . not as long as they'd have to stand in line at the INS gates where the contents of their luggage would be tossed around and their ID would be checked against computer files.

Computers! They were always going down. What if there was some computer glitch at the airport? Great. Cade could be in some interrogation room for hours, for days . . . trying to explain that the wrapped package in his bag was . . . a gift! A present for the girl he loved!

Loved? Delete that —

Alex had begun to do her own mumbling dance.

Breathe, a calming voice told her.

It wasn't Cam's, not today.

But it wasn't exactly not Cam's, either.

You can't think when you're hyperventilating. No oxygen to the brain. Breathe, Artemis.

Alex stopped pacing. Although she doubted it would net results, she couldn't help looking around. People of every color and kind were crowding the international area. Alex searched above heads covered by turbans, yarmulkes, head scarves, and broad-brimmed Aussie outback hats.

Then she saw her.

One arm raised in a loving wave, the other tightly

clutching an old book. Though it was bound in cracked brown leather, the book seemed to be radiating light.

A wisp of white robe, a toss of gleaming auburn hair, a flash of smiling gray eyes, and Miranda swept out of the terminal.

Alex rubbed her eyes. How stressed was she?

Was that really Coventry Mom? What was she doing in Boston? At the airport? And what was that crusty volume she was carrying?

Maybe Cam would find out since their equal-op mom seemed to be heading in her direction.

And not a minute too soon, Alex decided. It was her sister, after all, who needed the most help today. Cam was losing what Alex was gaining: a honey to hang with —

Unless Cade thought they were just . . . friends? Sure, why not? He hadn't used the L-word. Hadn't signed his e-mails with XXXs.

All at once, she turned. It felt as if two hands had gripped her shoulders and pointed her at the entrance to the international arrivals gate.

The double doors swung open behind the thrust of a luggage cart. The guy pushing it had curly black hair, dark glasses, and a soul patch sprouting in the cleft between his full lower lip and his strong, squared-off chin.

Cade!

Even without the motorcycle jacket and beat-up stovepipe jeans, she'd have known him. But would he recognize her?

Cade took off his dark glasses. His spotlight baby blues roamed the area. He'd looked right past her!

Wave, Alex, she told herself. *Hands up. Speak. Shout.* But her arms hung limply at her side and her lips had turned to Velcro.

Which wasn't so bad. 'Cause Cade's mouth had, too.

At least that was what it felt like after he abandoned his cart and raced through the crowd to catch her up in his arms and fasten his own Velcro lips to hers in a wonderfully familiar, yet wildly new kiss.

Arms around each other, Cade and Alex were on their way to pick up Cam, could actually see her ahead, her arm around Jason's high waist, when the commotion erupted. The entire area between the two couples was suddenly flooded with noise and light.

Flashbulbs popped. Video cameras whirred. Microphones were being lifted and shoved toward the center of the moving mob.

"What's going on?" Cade asked, straining like everyone around them to see who or what was in the middle of the melee.

T'Witches, hello. May I have your attention, please?

Alex and Cam got the message at exactly the same time.

Ileana!

"Someone said Brice Stanley is here," an excited woman told Cade. She was jumping up and down, trying to catch a glimpse of the superstar over the heads of the frantic media.

"Who's the babe?" a news guy shouted.

"It's his steady — the mystery blond," a cameraman called out from the inner circle. "Guess they kissed and made up."

"D'ja find out where they're going?"

Brice and I are on our way to Maui. It was Ileana again. *Your mother is around here somewhere. I told her not to bother seeing us off, but she insisted. Wanted to catch a glimpse of her baby girls before heading home. Don't worry, I won't be gone long. And when I do get back, Miranda and I have an important matter we'll need to discuss with you. Try to stay out of trouble. There'll be trouble enough to deal with when I return —*

"Hey, I just got here and you just left," Cade teased. Alex hadn't realized how raptly she'd been listening to Ileana. She gave Cade a smile she hoped was reassuring and turned to look at Cam.

Jason was staring adoringly at her sister, but her

twin's gray eyes, like her own, were focused on their mirror image.

An important matter to discuss? Alex repeated Ileana's words.

Trouble enough to deal with? Cam sent back.

The ominous phrases flew across the space that separated them, sounding serious and menacing.

What more was there to find out? What more was there to fear? Staying out of trouble didn't seem like an option, just a fragile hope.

Jason squeezed Cam's shoulder and she turned to look at him. Unexpectedly, tears gathered in her eyes again. She didn't want to lose him, not now. She didn't want anything to change. For this single moment she felt safe.

Glancing again at Alex, it occurred to her that the person she had grown closest to in the world was not leaving. Alex would be here for her. And she would be her sister's rock. They were T'Witches after all. No matter that one was saying good-bye while the other was saying hello. They were connected. And connection — to people they loved, whether near or living only in their hearts — was what would keep them safe.

No one, nothing, could break Camryn and Alex. Not while they were all about doing good and healing. And not while they were together.

EPILOGUE
THE GUARDIAN

The moment Ileana and Miranda had left his office, Thantos had turned on Sersee, grabbing the insolent girl by the throat.

Stunned, she had struggled in his grasp. The hulking warlock's iron grip made it impossible for her to speak. She sent him a desperate thought message: *I stole the book for you. I know what is in it. And still I wish to serve you.*

Contempt and curiosity shone in the fierce black eyes that stared at her. "You wish to serve me?" Thantos showed not a scrap of surprise nor a moment's hesitation. "Call off your dogs," he rasped at her, swinging her around so that her face was at the broken window and she could see the witch hunters marching beneath them.

Release me, she silently urged.

Her brazenness impressed and offended but did not surprise him.

"You wish to serve me?" Thantos's face was as raw and rageful as his voice. "Show me why I need one such as you, a fugitive fledgling who hides underground. A discarded child who scrabbles like a diseased rat through the caves of Coventry, sacred caves where once fierce witches and renegade spirits ruled. Why would I waste my time guiding the leader of a ragtag band of unruly runaways and uninitiated urchins? Show me why, Sersee," he challenged her, "and I will become your guardian. Fail me, imp, and you are dead."

He dropped her. And finally she surprised him.

He recognized the scent of the herbs she rubbed between her hands. He knew which crystals she'd chosen from the leather pouch under her cape. He watched as she performed a ritual he vaguely remembered, calling up a spell — both primitive and powerful — that he'd learned decades ago. It was a spell uninitiated rabble like Sersee should not have known.

Ignoring him, she tossed down the crystals, blew away the herbs, then leaned forward, her hands on the windowsill. Oblivious to the sharp shreds of glass against her palms, she stared down at the mob she'd sent to badger him.

The embarrassing threats bellowed from below faded.

One by one, the robed men looked up at Sersee.

Whispering incantations, she caught their eyes, smiling as they tried frantically to look away.

The black-bearded warlock watched as the fools removed their hoods in a stupor, mechanically, obediently. Some stepped back; some sat down dazed on the lawn they'd trashed; others rolled forward clutching their stomachs.

When all were sick and silenced, Sersee turned to face him. A cold breeze stirred the girl's tangled black hair. Her deep violet eyes flashed with satisfaction. The hint of a proud smile crossed her lips.

Slowly, slyly, she knelt before the brutal warlock. "Your enemies are my enemies, Lord Thantos," she said.

ABOUT THE AUTHORS

H.B. Gilmour is the author of numerous best-selling books for adults and young readers, including the *Clueless* movie novelization and series; *Pretty in Pink,* a University of Iowa Best Book for Young Readers; and *Godzilla,* a Nickelodeon Kids Choice nominee. She also cowrote the award-winning screenplay *Tag.*

H.B. lives in upstate New York with her husband, John Johann, and their yellow lab, Harry, one of the family's five dogs, five cats, two snakes (a boa constrictor and a python), and five extremely bright, animal-loving children.

Randi Reisfeld has written many best-sellers, such as the *Clueless* series (which she wrote with H.B.), the *Moesha* series, and biographies of Prince William, New Kids on the Block, and Hanson. Her Scholastic paperback *Got Issues Much?* was named an ALA Best Book for Reluctant Readers in 1999.

Randi has always been fascinated with the randomness of life. . . . About how any of our lives can simply "turn on a dime" and instantly (snap!) be forever changed. About the power each one of us has deep inside, if only we knew how to access it. About how any of us would react if, out of the blue, we came face-to-face with our exact double.

From those random fascinations, T*Witches was born.

Oh, and BTW: She has no twin (that she knows of) but an extremely cool family and a cadre of bffs to whom she is totally devoted.

MEET THE
TⓄWITCHES

Camryn Barnes—Smart, upbeat, and popular, Cam is best of breed all around. Except for one bone-chilling secret: Cam sees things happening before they happen. Very bad things.

Alexandra Fielding—Spunky, punky, and sarcastic, Alex is all about making it from day to day. Life's tough, but Alex deals. Except for the weirdness. Alex hears things. The things people think but haven't said.

HAVE YOU READ ALL THE BOOKS IN THE T⊙WITCHES SERIES?

T⊙WITCHES #1: *THE POWER OF TWO*

Identical twins. Separated at birth. For one very good reason . . .

If they ever met, they could combine their powerful gifts and help people, maybe even save a life. They could figure out who they really are and who their parents really are — or were. And they could fall into very evil hands. Guess what? They're about to meet.

T⊙WITCHES #2: *BUILDING A MYSTERY*

Alex and Cam finally learn some secrets about their past. But they still have a lot to uncover. Fortunately, there's new eye candy in town to keep the girls' minds off their troubles. Cade is dark and beautiful and seems to have secrets of his own. Alex is lured in . . . and it takes both girls to break his spell. But are they strong enough to hold back the evil that surrounds them?

T☉WITCHES #3: *SEEING IS DECEIVING*

Cam's and Alex's powers are getting in sync, and the twins can't help themselves. They're reading people's minds, using magick on the soccer field. It's bringing them closer together. But it's forcing Cam and her bff, Beth, apart.

When Alex sneaks out to an all-night party, she suddenly finds Beth — and herself — in terrible danger. Thantos, the evil one who wants the twins eliminated, has taken Beth hostage. Must Alex sacrifice herself to save her sister and her friend?

T☉WITCHES #4: *DEAD WRONG*

Alex's skeevy stepdad has resurfaced . . . and he wants Alex back. Like, for good. And Evan, Alex's Montana bud, is crashing. He needs help, stat. Time to 180 to Alex's hometown.

But there's more trouble in Montana than the twins ever expected. The powerful warlock Thantos has followed Cam and Alex. And he has a present for them. One that's six feet under.

ⓉWITCHES #5: *DON'T THINK TWICE*

Cam's best, Bree, is unraveling, and Cam feels locked out. Not so for Alex, who has been breaking into people's minds. She knows all Bree's secrets. But before the twins can help Bree, she is taken away. To a private place, for serious help.

There, Bree meets a mysterious woman who is able to heal her like no one else. But this woman is more than a stranger. She holds the key to everything that Cam and Alex have been searching for. If only they can get to her.

ⓉWITCHES #6: *DOUBLE JEOPARDY*

Miranda. The mother Cam and Alex never knew they had. A magnificent witch from the most powerful family on Coventry Island.

Rewind.

Locked away in a sanitarium the twins' whole lives, Miranda is broken. Physically and spiritually. And her freedom comes with a price. Cam and Alex will have to part with something that means more to them than they ever imagined.

And for once, their guardians can't help them.

T*WITCHES #7: *KINDRED SPIRITS*

Coventry Island. A lush, hidden world of magick and sorcery. It's where Cam and Alex were born. And it's where they're headed now. At last.

But Coventry doesn't feel much like home. A group of cooler-than-thou teen witches and warlocks aren't exactly making nice with the twins. And if Cam and Alex feel like the odd girls out in this place . . . where is it that they *really* belong?

Look for

◉WITCHES #9

SPLIT DECISION

Be careful.

No one had to warn Alex. It was all she'd been telling herself, again and again, since Cade, the super-crush, had come loping back into her life. Don't get in so deep that you can't get out. Leave an emotional escape hatch. Do not — she pictured road signs, as she pedaled her bike along the outskirts of Marble Bay — yield, or let your defenses down. Do not let him get to you. Do not expose your heart. It's too —

"Earth to Alex —"

— Fragile. Too late. *Kaboom!* She'd already fallen.

Cade was riding beside her, their wheels, Alex noted, rotating in sync. "If I were a mind reader —" he said with a mischievous twinkle in his cobalt eyes.

Alex gripped the handlebars so tightly, her knuckles turned white.

"— I would know why you've got that determined look on your face. Why your eyebrows are knitted in concentration, your lips pursed. Why we're biking side by side, yet you haven't heard a word I've said."

He'd been *talking* to her? Hyper-hearing girl? "Oh, man," she moaned, "my bad. Would you buy that I'm trying to memorize the Pythagorean theorem?"

"From anyone else? No. But if *you're* sellin', I'm buyin'." He winked.

She turned away. Not so he wouldn't see her blush. To stop the free fall she was in.

Alex had met Cade Richman last semester, when they'd been the new kids at Marble Bay High. Their connection went deeper than that.

There was insta-chemistry. Attraction at first sight.

And language arts. They totally got each other.

And biology, *if* that could be measured by just one kiss.

But not enough history. His dad had gotten transferred to Paris, and Cade, only sixteen, had gone with him.

With Cade went Alex's heart.

Fast forward. The boy with the dark, curly hair, greenish-blue eyes, and lopsided smile was back. For a summer cameo or for good? The question hung in the air between them. He hadn't said, and she was afraid to ask. Reading his mind was not an option, either. She banned herself from reading his mind. For her own sake, not his.

Be in the moment. That's how Cam's friend Amanda once put it. Don't think ahead. Don't think back. Feel, absorb everything that's happening now. Okay, she'd play.

Now, the sky above was pink, illuminating the few sunlit clouds. Now, the breeze was playing with her choppy purple hair, tangling it. Now, she peered at the boy riding in tandem with her. His inky curls were longer than she remembered, covering his neck. His lean frame was hunched forward on a borrowed bike that was much too small for him. Alex's keen sense of smell was one of her witch powers. Cade smelled of fresh, clean soap and a tinge of leather.

There was a special spot, Cade had told her, a place he used to go on the outskirts of town, when he just needed to be alone. Getting there was a trek, but the idea of its out-of-the-way-ness suited Alex.

As for the steep uphill part of the trek, that was another story. There was no trail to follow, but Cade knew where he was going. They'd had to drag their bikes along up what felt like a ninety-degree angle for the last part of the hike.

"It's worth it, I promise," Cade said, responding to Alex's huffing and puffing.

Straight up. That's how the boy was telling it. Cade's special spot was truly awesome, in the retro sense of that word. They ended up in a field, atop what was probably the highest peak around. It afforded the ultimate "scenic view." The navy-blue ocean straight ahead, the turquoise bay to the right, to the left, the green, forested landscape, and in the valley behind them, the town of Marble Bay.

"You like?" Cade asked.

"I do," Alex said softly, her breathing coming back to normal. "How'd you find this place? Remote doesn't begin to describe it."

He considered. "Sometimes, I think this place found me. Would you buy that?"

It was Alex's turn to grin. "If you're sellin' it . . ."

They'd spread a blanket out and gazed up at the now cloudless pure-blue sky. A kind of tension-be-gone washed over them; the sun kissed their faces. The only sounds were buzzing bees, chirpy birds, butterflies, cicadas . . . and, after a while, a low rumbling? Coming from Cade's abs? Alex couldn't suppress a giggle.

"You heard that?" Cade was embarrassed.

"Chill," she said. "I'm hungry, too. And, I came equipped."

Alex opened her backpack and withdrew a pile of plastic containers. She'd prepared salad, tuna, cheese, bread, fruit, chips, and bottled water.

Cade whistled in appreciation. "That's what's so cool about you. You're unpredictable. Not what people expect —"

Alex stopped what she was doing and folded her arms. He so wasn't getting away with that comment.

"Let's see, purple hair, random piercings, studded cuffs, and trend-aversity render me unable to make a sandwich? That what you mean?"

"Busted," he admitted sheepishly.

"It's my suburban sister who's totally kitchen-phobic. That girl thinks adding strawberries to Special K is gourmet cooking. Speaking of walking contradictions — looked into a mirror lately?"

Cade was the kid who'd come to school looking rough, raggedy, and, at first, secretive. Nothing to suggest the rich boy this Richman really was. "I never did ask you," Alex gave voice to her thoughts. "Why'd you hide who you really were?"

Cade leaned over on his elbow. Their faces were inches apart. "I didn't. This is who I really am. You were the only girl who ever got it. Besides, we all have secrets —"

"Not me," Alex lied. "I'm an open book. Ask me anything."

He did. Which is how they spent the early afternoon, talking, laughing, trading tales, breaking bread, realizing how little — yet how much — they knew about each other. Even leaving out the witch part, Alex felt like she could talk to him forever. And listen, too.

Check it, in comparison to Cade, Alex's life had been relatively stable. His dad was some big muckety-muck in a global conglom, and the family moved often. In his sixteen-plus years, Cade could count as many schools. Finishing his sophomore year in Paris had been his first experience in another country. He noted, "The city of lights, they call it. And it is cool, but definitely not the perfect city people dream of."

Alex had never dreamed about Paris — her own dreams had been more modest. As in: getting out of the trailer, wishing her mom wouldn't be sick . . . and understanding her weirdness. Well, she figured, two out of three ain't bad. It was the one she wasn't able to do that still gnawed at her.

Needing to pull herself out of the looming gloom, she asked quickly, "Did you learn to speak French?"

"A little. I went to the American School, so the classes were all in English. Besides, French is the language of love — and well, I didn't get to practice much."

Alex couldn't meet his eyes. She was wading into way dangerous waters. Eyes cast downward, she urged, "Say something in French."

A sly smile crossed his lips. "Okay, here goes. *Tu es très jolie, Alex, mon petit chou*." It came out, "Too ay tray joe lee, Ah-lex, ma petite shoo."

"Sounds romantic. What's it mean?" she asked.

He cupped her chin. "You are so pretty . . ."

She smiled.

"— my little cabbage!"

Alex scrunched her face and mock punched him. "I walked right into that one, didn't I?"

Cade answered by reaching over, putting his arm around her shoulders. "You want romantic? How about this?" He pulled her close.

Shane had come for her. Cam was a goner.

She was premonition girl. She was hyper-sense girl — but Cam had no warning, no inkling she'd feel so strongly and act so rashly. She didn't demand the explanation he so owed her. Her mind closed down, and her heart opened up. His arms were outstretched. She rushed into them. As fools rush in. Or, to paraphrase an historical cliché, Cam thought, "He came, she saw, he conquered."

The massive mahogany doorway of Crailmore, meant to humble those who passed through it, did not diminish Shane Wright. Rather, it framed him, as if he were a princely portrait of regal bearing. He was almost posed, Cam thought fleetingly, hands on hips, legs astride, shiny blond hair that fell to his shoulders. Upon those shoulders rested a cape of deep indigo. Had he worn it on purpose, the purpose being to bring out his blueberry eyes?

She felt like one big protoplasm of mush. Evidenced by the thudding of her heart, fluttering moth wings in her tummy, and stupid smile she could not wipe off her face. Playing it cool was not an option. Not when Shane was so hot.

"You're here" was all he said, holding her tightly and sighing with relief. Had he doubted she would come? He needn't have worried. That famous movie line flashed through her head: "You had me at hello."

Shane brushed away her bangs and kissed her lightly on her forehead. "Come," he whispered, "with me."

No way, buster. Not until you come inside and offer up some real explanation for your betrayal. Not until you tell it to my face, to my mother's face — for all I know someone else was writing those e-mails. I'm not taking a step with you until you prove to both of us you've changed.

So that's what Cam should have said.

Only, how could she? When, just then, his hand — solid, soft, comforting — closed over hers. Their fingers entwined as if acting independently and out of habit. They walked silently down the steps, along the walkway, and through the iron gates that surrounded the mansion.

She'd been so wrapped up in her feelings that Cam hadn't noticed the large black horse tethered to one of the spikes of the gate. It wasn't until Shane pulled her toward it that Cam squeaked, "What's *that* doing here?"

"That is a stallion," Shane explained proudly, reaching up to stroke its silky black mane.

Cam backed away. In theory, she considered herself a friend to all creatures great and small, but in reality, when the really big ones got so up close and personal you could feel its hot breath on you? That's where "friendship" ended.

"This is Epony," Shane was saying, stroking the horse's snout. "He looks fierce, but he wouldn't hurt a tadpole."

"How's he feel about humans?" Cam asked, remembering with a sick feeling her first — and only — experience atop a horse. Her family had vacationed at a dude ranch one summer. Cam was about seven, before she knew she was a witch or what her premonitions meant. Had she known, she would have refused to mount the old mare she'd been assigned to. She looked gentle enough, but Cam knew she wasn't. Cam had felt chilled and nervous; her eyes went blurry and she saw the mare bucking; she saw herself flying through the air. But who could she tell? By that age, she already knew her parents would laugh it off, go all cliché about facing her fears.

Trying to be brave, she'd finally allowed herself to be hoisted up. She hadn't been on ol' Bessie's back more than a few minutes, when the critter freaked out, tore off in a gallop, bucked, and rid itself of her. Cam was unhurt only because she'd expected the fall, was prepared for it. When it came, she managed to break it with her arms. Otherwise, the fall might have cracked open her skull.

Warily, Cam regarded this animal. Epony was ink-jet-black, from his bushy tail to his bulging eyes, evil-looking orbs, staring straight at her. She wanted to turn away, but Shane's arms were around her shoulders, pulling her closer gently.

"Make friends with him. He likes to be petted." Shane guided her hand across the horse's neck. It was taut, muscular, and scratchy, like burnt weeds.

"What's he . . . doing here?"

Shane untied the reins. "*He* is our ride to the coastline. Aren't you, boy?"

"Can't we walk?" The brief time Cam had spent on Coventry, she'd walked everywhere. So had everyone else.

Shane shook his head. "Too far."

"And cars are —?"

"Too mainland."

"So, skateboard, Rollerblades, scooters, bus, train, Lear jet . . . ?"

"Horses," Shane told her, "played an important part in our history. Black ones, like Epony, symbolized power and vitality."

Shane was something of a Coventry know-it-all. The last time Cam had been on Coventry, he'd taught her the island's origins as an underground railroad, a refuge for persecuted witches. Ever since, the island had proved a magnet for others, good people with highly developed paranormal skills. It had evolved organically into a home-land, a safe place to live in peace and learn the lessons of healing and helping others. Cam did not remember any mention of Black Beauty here.

"Give me your foot," Shane instructed. "We keep certain traditions alive, especially when they're useful. Besides, this big guy comes from a long line of Coventry thoroughbreds. No one taught you about that? You never heard the name Epony before?" He looked at Cam with real curiosity. As if this was not a rhetorical question.

"That would be a no. And no."

"I'll teach you, then," Shane said, a trace of satisfaction in his voice, as he placed Cam's sneakered foot inside the stirrup. "Up ya go. Hold on to the saddle horn." He boosted her onto the saddle. "I won't let you get hurt."

A rebel brain cell poked out of its corner and made itself heard: Hello! Déjà vu, anyone? Sequel-itis? He's lied to you before. You trusted him, he betrayed you.

But Cam felt no bad vibes, no sense of foreboding that Shane was leading her, via horseback, into a trap. She put her instincts ahead of her good sense.

She squirmed in the saddle, but when Shane hoisted himself up behind her and encircled her waist, her instincts told her to relax.

Shane grasped the reins. "Come on, boy, let's go." He nudged with his boots, directing the horse forward. Cam clenched her legs tight around the animal and gripped the saddle horn. The young warlock held Epony to a slow pace as they trotted through the countryside surrounding Crailmore and then into the deep woods behind the estate.

They were headed to Coventry's north shore when Shane told her, "It's usually pretty deserted, since there are no beaches or ferry docks."

"The shore less traveled?" Cam was being cute, but the poetry-check was lost on him.

In all earnestness he continued, "You should see it. After all, you own it."

"I what?" Cam looked over her shoulder at him.

"All this." He nodded straight ahead as they emerged from the woods toward a rocky shore. "This is all DuBaer property. It's yours."

"No," she corrected. "It belongs to Lord Thantos."

"Your uncle," Shane pointed out.

"Unfortunately," she mumbled.

They'd ridden as far as they could take the horse, near the edge of a clifflike drop-off. Dismounting, they left the animal on flat ground and headed, hand in hand, down a rocky slope, sometimes balancing precariously on the sharp edges of granite formed by decades of wind and mist rising off the Great Lake. Cam, a natural athlete, turned out to be more agile than Shane. She'd taken the lead and helped him negotiate the sea-battered rocky terrain until they reached the shoreline. It was cooler and windier on this part of the island, and Cam was glad she'd worn a scrunchie as a bracelet. Once the hair was out of her eyes, she surveyed the view. It was spectacular. Lake Superior stretched before them, tiny ripples of waves made squiggles on the water, the midday sun reflected off its glasslike surface.

Shane had not brought her here to admire the scenery or even behold all that she "owned." He knew what Cam needed to hear. He wasted no time cutting to the chase, smoothly, confidently, almost as if he'd rehearsed it. . . .